THE GEEK JOB

EROTIC PARANORMAL ROMANCE

EVE LANGLAIS

CHAPTER ONE

"I DON'T WORK the evening of or morning after a full moon." She began the negotiations with an aloof smile, casually seated in a leather covered club chair, her steel toed boots propped on top of a marble topped desk.

The dark haired vampire with full sensual lips and dark eyes—handsome if she could ignore his walking corpse status—touched his fingertips together to form a steeple and leaned back in his chair. "The job I have in mind will be occurring this coming weekend, so that won't be an issue. What else?"

Lexie couldn't hold back a cocky grin as she recited her list of demands. "I work alone. While you can have other guards discreetly stationed, they are not to approach me or interfere with my target. You will provide a cleanup crew for any messes that occur during my protection of the target. In case I'm injured while protecting my assign-ment, you will ensure I receive immediate and first class medical care. I will study the file and provide an additional list of requirements, at your expense of course. As for my fees, it'll cost you fifteen thousand for the weekend, consisting of no more than seventy two hours. That number could go up if the subject proves difficult. I expect to see the full amount deposited to my Paypal account no later than eight a.m. the day I begin the task. Oh, and I also want four, front row tickets to the next UFC match in Vegas." She threw that last bit in just for fun.

The vampire arched a brow. "You think highly of yourself, don't you?"

She leaned forward and her leather jacket gaped open to flash the cleavage clearly visible through the gaping neckline of her tank top, a calculated ploy that grabbed her prospective employer's attention. *Dead or not, all men are the same.* "For what you're asking, I think you're getting my services cheap. I mean, guarding some science dweeb is all well and good, but to pretend to be some normal human ditz and shack up with him as his girlfriend, which I might add will require me putting out... Damn, given what a high class call girl goes for these days, I should be asking for more."

Frederick Thibodeaux, the vampire who'd called her in for the job interview, gave her a pained look. "You'd better be worth what you're asking for, Lexington. Do you know how many strings I'm going to have to pull to get those tickets?"

Lexington, who preferred to go by her nickname Lexie, smirked. "That's the price you pay if you want to engage my golden pussy and talent. So, do we have a deal?" She'd worked with Frederick before and knew he'd cave to her demands. He just liked to beat around the bush and fake hardship before he sealed the deal.

"Let's make sure you've got the details of the job straight. You are to befriend the good doctor as he arrives for the conference. In other words, finagle your way back to his room. Once you've got him pussy whipped, you are to stay glued by his side the entire length of the conference, doing whatever you need to keep him happy and oblivious. I want him returned without any holes or scratches he didn't own already. Your task ends once he gets into the limo for the airport, taking him back to my property and his lab."

"Wouldn't this whole task be easier if you told him what we were, thus allowing us to guard him openly?" Lexie didn't have a problem with the fact she needed to sleep with the guy. The nerdy types tended to work harder for it in bed, and not take as long doing it. However, she found it hard to bend her mind around the fact Frederick had a geek working on a solution to the vampire sun allergy issue without letting the nerdazoid know vampires were involved. How the hell was that supposed to work? Not that she cared, but curiosity made her ask.

Frederick made a moue of annoyance. "Unfortunately, our resident scientist has proven skittish in the past. We let our secret slip by accident once before with almost catastrophic consequences."

Lexie snorted. "He caught one of you guys munching on someone, didn't he?"

Frederick smiled coldly. "We don't take kindly to trespassers. Unfortunately, given the bloody methods we use to set an example, our scientist had a minor gibbering meltdown when he came across it during one of his nocturnal walks, walks that I might add we've since banned. We managed to wipe that unfortunate incident, but as you well know, too much messing around in a humans brain, and...poof. He'll end up a vegetable. And given how close he is to solving our dilemma, his remarkable brain must be protected at all cost."

"So why even let him go to that conference? Can't you just like, forbid him or something as his boss?"

"We've tried to dissuade him; however, because of some scientific paper he wrote, he was asked to act as a speaker. Some great honor apparently. He was quite adamant about attending."

Lexie stopped attempting to dissuade her employer. She rather looked forward to the assignment even if she had to put up with a few minutes of groping and grunting. Besides, she needed a vacation and what better time or place than at a five star hotel with free food, money and the UFC tickets she coveted. "What kind of opposition can I expect?"

"The usual—rival clans looking to steal him, even more so since an ex-employee leaked secrets about his work. The Fae also want to eliminate him because they fear us embracing the day, and then there are the assassins, like yourself, who have probably been offered a bounty to capture him, dead or alive."

Lexie whistled. "Sounds like fun." And she wouldn't mind the exercise to her skills. "Now, while I'm working as his shadow, I am going to assume you'll have men stationed throughout the conference area scanning for suspects."

"Correct. You won't see them, but they'll see you." The leer on the vampire's face made her roll her eyes.

"If he's as geeky as you say, then they won't see much because I doubt it will take more than a minute to please your little scientist and put him to sleep. And besides, you seem to forget, nudity is my preferred state." Werewolves scoffed at the hang ups other beings held about the naked body. Given how the change tore through anything they wore, many shifters preferred to wear little to no clothing and didn't care who saw them in their natural state.

"So we're agreed then?" Frederick asked as he stood.

Lexie also got to her feet and held out her hand. "Consider me your geek's new girlfriend." They shook and sealed the deal.

Time to pack.

She left the vampire's mansion with a folder tucked into her knapsack, additional information on her target. She straddled her sport bike and put on her helmet, not because she feared injuring herself, but because human cops could be dicks about their stupid laws.

The half-moon teased her in the sky and made her inner wolf rumble knowing the full one soon approached.

Until she could run wild through the woods, the night air ruffling her fur as she hunted, she'd make do with the speed on her bike.

She started the engine, enjoying the rumbling vibration of all that power between her legs. Put a cock on the seat and she'd probably enjoy herself more than she managed with a man. With a chuckle to herself, she gunned the bike and, with a squeal of spinning tires, took off for home.

As she weaved her bike in and out of the sparse traffic that flowed this time of night, she pondered her assignment. It wouldn't be the first time she had to seduce a target. Her nonchalance about it was one of the reasons her services were in such high demand and fetched a pretty penny. She refused to look at it as whoring herself, more like scratching an itch while getting paid. She saw no shame in admitting she had needs only another body —preferably male—could take care of. What that male looked like didn't truly matter in the scheme of things, that's what light switches and paper bags existed for. As long as he had a dick and a tongue, any man could do the job. She wasn't one to get hung up on girly notions of love and relationships. She truly was a lone wolf compared to the other bitches of her kind.

Most female wolves were submissive, rolling over and showing their belly to the first interested male. Lexie, however, possessed alpha tendencies. She refused to cower for any male, not exactly a popular trait for a female in a society where packs were ruled by men. So, she'd left rather than kill the annoying males who'd thought to cow her into their preconceived notion of a she-wolf. And she wasn't invited back despite her poor mother's pleas. The male wolves she'd maimed were apparently still pissed at her for showing them, with violent means, that no meant no.

Alone, without a pack or family to support her—her father disowning his unnatural daughter—she struggled to make ends meet with job after job. She discovered there weren't many career opportunities for a girl like her. Well, not ones that paid the money she needed to live comfortably. She fell into her calling quite by accident, saving the daughter of a business man who'd just joined the vampiric ranks. He rewarded her and began throwing jobs her way along with referrals which was how she encountered Frederick.

Security work fit her perfectly because she had the muscle, the brains and the cunning to make a great bodyguard. As her special status became known among certain groups, they'd added to her repertoire of uses—killer, spy, personal guard, and undercover agent. She did it all in the name of her dream retirement—all that was, except the killing of young'uns and the innocent. Her perverse moral code wouldn't allow her to stoop that low. But ask her to stake a rogue vamp gone wild and she was there in her leathers. If a rabid wolf required putting down, she owned a shot gun loaded with silver shot for the job. No matter the task, she prevailed, and she loved every minute of it.

This newest assignment, which she'd nicknamed to herself *The Geek Job*, sounded almost like a vacation compared to her usual stuff, a much needed weekend of relaxation. She just hoped her target wasn't paper bag ugly because she hadn't enjoyed dick in a while and her pussy had no qualms complaining about the fact it was long overdue.

Arriving at her townhouse, she flicked the button on her key fob dangling from the ignition and the garage door opened. She slid in and dismounted her bike after flicking the kickstand forward. She strode into her home and tossed her backpack on the kitchen island. She stripped off her leathers, hanging them over a chair, not stopping until she got down to her panties. She kept the place warm so she didn't even shiver in her almost nude state. She only kept her bottoms on to preserve her couch. Coochie stains on the furniture just didn't scream class.

She unzipped her knapsack and brought the folder along with a beer into her bedroom. She flopped onto her king-sized bed and began to read. Frederick had provided a thorough background on her geek, and she sipped her beer as she perused the file.

Name: Anthony Dominic Savell

Born: September 19, 1979

Height: 76 inches

Weight: 95 kg

Hair: Brown

Eyes: Blue (wears glasses)

Orientation: Heterosexual

Other info: Graduated high school with honors at the age of fourteen. Went on to university with scholarships and obtained numerous degrees in the fields of biology, medicine, science, chemistry. Went to work for a private research corporation in 2005. Offered a lab with anything he wanted, on site residence in 2008.

Lexie fought a yawn as she read through the dull biography. Boring. It sounded like her geek didn't have a life outside of his work and research. She rifled through the rest of the papers looking for anything interesting about her target, but found nothing, not even mention of a girlfriend. Mind numbing as she found the info, she needed to study it and his reason for going to the conference. While she planned to play the part of seductive science groupie, she would still need to know a little bit about him. At the very bottom of the pile she finally found a picture, more like an employee mug shot, but it gave her a face for her nerd. He sported shaggy, brownish un-kept hair, dark rimmed glasses and a slightly startled look which seemed at odds with his square chin and sensual lips. *Well, at least he's not butt ugly.*

His height and weight also put him on the larger size, which would work out in her favor. *Nothing worse than breaking a fragile human when you're trying to get them off.* The human boy she'd accidentally maimed in high school eventually regained use of his legs, and she became more careful with her affections when dealing with humans. A shame because she really did enjoy going wild and unrestrained in the bedroom—biting and scratching totally turning her on—however, only another Lycan or supernatural could handle her passion when she let loose. Unfortunately, shifter lovers tended to try and mark her, making them unsuitable for bedding.

Although few tried that anymore since word had gotten out about Derrick. She still wasn't allowed anywhere near Tennessee, where one-eyed Derrick ruled the packs since his father's demise. She'd warned him though, not her fault he refused to listen.

As she snuggled into her comforter, she made a mental list of the things she'd need to pack for her trip—slutty business suits, thongs, flats so she didn't tower, nylons and garters, her Browning High Power loaded with silver bullets, her stakes, ooh and her vibrator in case her geek came before the main event.

With a snicker at her last thought, she slipped into sleep.

CHAPTER TWO

ANTHONY PUSHED his glasses back up on his nose as he stepped from the cab that deposited him outside the hotel housing the conference. He couldn't believe he'd made it. For the last three years, he'd buried himself in his work at Mr. Thibodeaux's lab. He'd shown little interest in leaving the property given the fascinating project he worked on, a project he'd reluctantly left to attend this conference, yet, how could he refuse? They'd selected his paper on DNA abnormalities where he'd theorized that a simple twist of a DNA strand could make a person's condition seem unreal, supernatural even, like Mr. Thibodeaux for example. The man exhibited a fatal allergy to the exposure of UV rays and required vast amounts of iron and blood transfusions to keep his body healthy. In times past, the superstitious masses would have condemned his employer as some unnatural creature, a vampire. Ridiculous, of course.

Mr. Thibodeaux suffered from an allergy which came about as a result of some warped DNA strands. A genetic anomaly was the culprit here, not mystical nonsense.

With science, he would prove monsters did not, in fact, exist and if all went well, he would cure them. Then—

A body jostled him as he stood woolgathering on the pavement; a feminine form whose tantalizing perfume made his saliva glands work overtime. How strange, given both his mind and body knew a woman didn't provide bodily sustenance.

"I'm awfully sorry for bumping into you like that." The sultry voice slid around him and, to his mortification, his cock twitched. *Surely it hasn't been that long since I've taken care of my bodily needs that my penis would show a sexual interest just from a voice?* He'd have to rectify his neglect later in the shower before he embarrassed himself.

Anthony had to look down to see the owner of the voice, his freakish height as always making him stand out, which made her not seeing him so odd. But he forgot all about her clumsy nature when he saw her.

Tall herself, even in the flats she wore, she gazed up at him in surprise. Anthony lost his train of thought, drawn into her soft green eyes flecked with brown. His gaze took in her lustrous brown hair caught up in an untidy chignon, and her proper, yet sensual, attire which consisted of a fitted cream jacket over a crimson blouse tucked into a pencil thin, black skirt. Her smooth, lightly tanned skin provided a perfect contrast to her pink glossed lips.

Humor glinted in her expression and her mouth tilted into a partial smile. Anthony struggled to regain control of himself and blushed as he realized she'd caught him staring. His heart sped up as he strove to find his voice in the face of the most beautiful woman he'd ever encountered. "Uh, no harm done. I guess I shouldn't have been blocking the sidewalk."

"No, it's my fault for not looking where I walked," she replied, her gaze not wavering from his, sending a shiver racing down his spine.

Her close proximity not only affected his lower regions, it made his pulse race. Anthony knew he needed to escape and regain his composure, then he'd need to figure out why one pretty woman flustered him so. "Um, well, I should get inside and get signed in." His genius in the lab, as usual, didn't extend to his banter.

"Are you also here for the conference?" she asked in a low tone that set his body tingling and made the blood in his brain rush elsewhere.

"Uh, yes. I'm actually one of the speakers." Anthony flushed at his boast.

"Really? How fantastic," she purred. "I'm here for just one of the speakers. I'm just dying to hear Anthony Savall talk. I read his paper on DNA and myth and just loved it. He is so brilliant."

Anthony's body suffused with heat and he wanted to reply, but his lips refused to move, mostly out of fear he'd say something dorky and scare her off. The confidence he enjoyed among his peers evaporated in the face of his immense attraction to her.

She didn't seem to notice anything amiss; although, he surely looked like the world's biggest doofus standing there like a mute.

"I guess I'll see you around." She smiled before she turned and strutted off with a wiggle that made Anthony close his eyes, hoping the blood in his penis would return to his brain. Thank science he wore baggy trousers and a long jacket.

He cursed his social ineptness at the prime opportunity, now lost, to introduce himself and ask the gorgeous woman to dinner. In a fantasy world, where he didn't turn into a stammering schoolboy, he would have swept her off her feet with his witty banter and smarts. He would have wined and dined her, all the while charming her with his intellect. At the end of the repast, she would have come back to his room where he would have worshipped every sun kissed inch of her body while she moaned his name.

Could have, should have. Anthony sighed. He was a researcher not a suave Casanova, and it didn't take a genius to realize his reality sucked.

CHAPTER THREE

LEXIE CHECKED in at the front desk, her room conveniently situated next to the giant scientist, a string that Frederick had pulled to ensure the ease of her task. As she waited for her room card, she pondered the geek she needed to protect. Turning part way, she could see him through the glass front doors, still standing outside. His dumbstruck expression warmed her.

While Anthony Savall looked the part of nerdy scientist with his pale complexion, large glasses and untidy hair, his height took her by surprise. Sure the report listed him at seventy-six inches, but for some reason she hadn't clued in that it would make him tower over her. In her world, geeks were supposed to be short and round shouldered, not freakishly tall next to her five foot nine. *And I didn't pack heels.* Expecting a shorter stature, slouching target, she'd packed her flats so as to not appear too imposing. *I wonder, if I can order up some heels?*

Another surprise was the fact her wolf showed an interest in the human, waking and staying attentive during their conversation. Strange, because her lupine side usually waited for blood and violence to rouse itself. She paid it no mind though. Who knew what intrigued her beast. Maybe it had scented the fact her skittish geek was prey—a male red riding hood to her big bad wolf. Lexie bit her lip so as to not snort at that last thought.

The desk clerk handed her a key card, his expression fawning. Lexie growled and giggled when the youth blanched.

With a wiggle she knew would turn heads, she made her way to the elevator. A sideways glance showed Anthony, who'd finally come in with bright cheeks, watching her. *Don't worry, my giant geek. You'll be seeing me again real soon.*

Lexie found her room and slid her key card in the slot. She stepped in and dropped her luggage. She quickly went to work, unlocking the door that adjoined her room to Anthony's in case of an emergency. She performed a rapid check of his quarters to ensure nothing dangerous waited to surprise her target, but saw nothing more menacing than a pillow mint, which she ate—her sweet tooth just couldn't resist. She didn't have time to sweep for bugs, but assumed their presence.

She slid back into her room, closing the now unlocked barrier. She unpacked her things as she waited for the next stage in her plan, using this moment of free time to hang her suits and arrange her toiletries. She also stashed her weapons around the room and used her keen sense of smell to scout out the cameras Frederick would have installed. Dead in body didn't mean dead in libido. She'd known the pervert would want a peek. He'd placed one in the bathroom and one by the bed. She left them for the moment. Forewarned, she could control what he'd get to see. Besides, an audience always added an extra element to sex.

Done with her preparation, she waited for her moment. With her enhanced shifter hearing, she had no problem making out her geek's actions next door. He unpacked, the sound of his suitcase zipper loud. Drawers opened and closed. Hangers rattled as he hung things. He left the bathroom door open as he peed, and then washed his hands. *A nerd with manners.*

He returned to his room and she strained to hear him. He mumbled to himself, something along the lines of "... she's just a pretty woman. No reason why I can't talk to her or ask her to dinner."

Lexie smiled. Apparently her first impression had stuck—good. So far her plan unfolded smoothly, not that she'd had any doubts. Men and their dicks were so predictable.

She ditched her jacket and slipped the top button of her blouse out of its loop, creating a shadowy vee. She waited to hear the sound of him opening his door into the hall before stepping out of her own room, and of course, turning with surprise etched on her face to greet him.

"Hi, there. What a coincidence meeting you again," she said brightly.

He looked startled—kind of like the deer she'd run

down on her last run through the woods. It was kind of cute.

"Um, hi."

She could judge by his reddening cheeks that he'd meant to say more, but shyness rendered him mute. "I was just going down to check into the conference. You know, get my name tag and a schedule of events. Then I was going to get some dinner. I know this is presumptuous, but I don't know anybody here and well..." She trailed off and gave him an expectant look.

"W-what?" he managed to stammer.

Lexie smiled at him coyly and restrained a giggle as she batted her lashes for good measure. "Would you have dinner with me?"

His jaw dropped, his surprise at her invitation clear. "I—uh-um. That is—"

Lexie dropped her eyes and schooled her features to look disappointed. "I knew it was silly of me to ask. You probably have plans already. I'm sorry to have bothered you." She started to turn slowly.

"No," he almost shouted. "I mean, yes, I would love to have dinner with you."

She pivoted back and beamed at him. "Oh, thank you. Shall we both go down then to get checked in? After, we can go straight to dinner? I'm *famished*." She inflected her last word and saw his eyes dilate behind his lenses. She didn't wait for him to answer this time. She wasn't sure he could, and honestly, it turned her on, her erotic effect on him strangely contagious. Something about him drew her, made her want to rip those glasses off his face and kiss him. *This job might turn out to be a lot more fun than I expected.* And apparently her body needed some exercise given its rousing interest in a geek whom she usually wouldn't have given a second glance.

She linked her arm around his—and found it surprisingly thick. A nerd who worked out? She couldn't wait to unwrap him later and find out.

At her urging, they made it to the elevator and rode it down in a thick silence. She could tell he wanted to talk, but every time her gaze met his, he blushed and looked away—and the bulge at his groin grew. His bulky clothes couldn't quite hide from someone with her developed powers of observation the fact her presence titillated him. It made her own panties dampen as her cleft reacted with pleasure. For a moment, she naughtily wondered what would happen if she were to press herself against him, right this very moment. *Probably faint,* snickered her mischievous mind.

She gave him a break and let go of his arm when they reached the lobby. However, she did nothing to control the wiggle in her walk as she made her way over to the sign in table. She waited until he was almost behind her to bend over and sign her name, thrusting her bottom out to accidentally bump him in the groin.

His strangled moan and rigid poke against her ass made her smile. She straightened and turned to face him, pretending she hadn't just felt his erection against her backside. She peeled her nametag off the wax backing and slapped it on her silk covered breast, holding in a smirk as his eyes couldn't help following her every movement. She rubbed the tag for good measure and saw him swallow. *Poor guy doesn't stand a chance.* "Your turn."

She moved aside and pretended to look around with interest. He signed in and only when he placed his name tag on did she exclaim, "Oh my god. You're Anthony Savell. Why didn't you say anything?"

Again his cheeks heated, but he managed to speak—finally. "I didn't want to appear like I was bragging."

"Why ever not? That piece you wrote in that journal a few months ago was brilliant. I can see we're going to have a fantastic time at dinner. I can't wait to pick your brain."

The smile he bestowed on her warmed her and, to her shock, tightened her nipples. The man had a killer grin when he used it. "Thanks for saying so. It's definitely an exciting field."

"And I can't wait to hear all about it over dinner and drinks."

She linked her arm in his again as they made their way to the hotel's restaurant. Phase one of the geek job was well underway, and it looked like phase two which involved getting into his room via his pants would actually be more fun than anticipated.

CHAPTER FOUR

ANTHONY WANTED TO PINCH HIMSELF. *I'm hallucinating.* He could think of no other explanation for how and why this beautiful woman ate dinner with him. Talking animatedly one minute, listening attentively the next, she managed to melt some of his shyness at her obvious interest in him, even if she tied his tongue in knots every time she touched him. Her hand kept reaching out to squeeze his, and each time it felt like she'd wrapped her hand around something else, something hard and throbbing, thankfully hidden by the table. He still didn't understand why she affected him so deeply. Never before had attraction to the opposite sex turned him into a blushing idiot, but at the same time, he loved it.

Logic stated that the woman's pheromones must be unusually developed or of a variety that truly appealed to him, but his dick didn't care about the biological science of it. It just wanted to bend her over the nearest table and pump her to orgasm. Anthony bit back a groan at the mental image and dug the tines of his fork into his leg, the pain reining in his raging, baser desire.

Lexie, his gorgeous dinner partner didn't seem to notice a thing amiss. She chattered away, inane talk that thankfully required little thought or input from him. Their waiter brought their entrees, and he looked forward to something to occupy him other than imagining how she'd look on her knees, peering up at him.

Anthony took a bite of his pasta then forgot to chew. Heck, he forgot to breathe, he became so caught up in watching Lexie enjoy her meal. She took a bite of her juicy, rare steak and closed her eyes with a groan. Her pleasure in her meal, the way she licked her fork, masticated with sensual satisfaction—it was the most erotic thing he'd ever watched and yet had nothing to do with sex.

She caught him watching and smiled. "I do so love a properly cooked steak." She gazed at his mostly uneaten meal. "Mmm, that pasta of yours looks yummy. Mind if I have a bite?" She reached forward and wrapped her hand around his. She drew his laden fork to her mouth and sucked the food off before releasing his hand. Anthony had no idea what his meal tasted like, but he regained interest after her lips covered his fork. Just knowing the tines had touched her mouth turned him on. *How pathetic am I?*

As the food on their plates—well, mostly hers—dwindled, a new waiter approached them with an open bottle of wine. Lexie, short for Lexington as she'd informed him, frowned at the man. "We didn't order this."

The waiter smiled with a lot of teeth that, for some reason, sent a chill down Anthony's spine. "It's a gift from an admirer," said the waiter with a heavy accent.

It was Anthony's turn to frown. *Is someone trying to hit on her?* Understandable given her beauty, but he didn't like it, which in turn, baffled him. He had no claim on her, so why the jealousy?

The waiter poured the ruby colored wine into their glass goblets, and then stood, as if waiting for them to try it. Anthony picked his up by the stem and inclined his head at her. "To not eating alone." He held his glass out in a toast.

She smiled and leaned forward to grab her own glass, but fumbled it instead, splashing the liquid across the front of her blouse. Lexie jumped up from her seat and grabbed a napkin to wipe with while the waiter fled, probably to get a cloth for cleaning. Anthony put down his wine and snatched up his own napkin, then, not thinking, began dabbing at her too. It only took him a few swipes to realize he was brushing her breasts and he snatched his hand back as if burned.

Mortified, he stammered. "I-I'm so sorry. I didn't mean—that is, I—"

She stepped close and shh-ed him. She grasped his hand and brought it back up, pressing it against her chest, her pebbled nipple evident through the wet silk. "I don't mind. Actually, can't you tell I enjoyed it?"

Anthony's cock tented his pants and he wanted to pull away in embarrassment, but she wouldn't let him. Instead, she pressed in even closer and lifted herself on tiptoe to brush her mouth across his. Anthony stopped breathing, afraid she'd realize she kissed a nerd.

"I need to get out of these clothes," she murmured against his mouth. "Care to help me?"

He didn't trust himself to speak aloud, not when his mind spun with pure gibberish, so instead, he nodded. She kissed him lightly on the lips again before sliding an arm around his waist. It seemed only natural he slide his arm around her back. Entwined like lovers—if he didn't fuck it up between here and the hotel room—they walked out of the restaurant to the elevators and he thanked the fact he'd signed to charge the dinner to his room at the start of the meal. He wanted nothing to interfere or delay his time with Lexie.

He feared breaking the spell tentatively spun between them, certain it would only take one word to make her change her mind. But as soon as the elevator doors closed, she proved her interest as she pressed her body against his while her mouth hotly latched onto his. He met her with a passion usually reserved for science, his body afire instead of his mind. He circled his arms around her, only mildly surprised at the wiry strength he felt in her frame.

The elevator arrived at their floor with a ding and they broke apart, both panting. Anthony couldn't believe the smoldering look in her eyes. *She wants me?* She licked her swollen lips and grabbed him by the hand, tugging him down the hall. She unlocked her door and dragged him inside. He'd no sooner shut the door behind him than she was on him, her mouth eagerly tasting his, her hands tugging at his belt.

Events began moving at the speed of light. He wanted to tell her to slow down. Her passion over-whelmed even as it flattered him. He didn't say a word, couldn't with his tongue caught in a tangle with hers. Although, he did grunt when she freed his cock and wrapped her hand around it. She stroked him, sliding her hand from tip to base and Anthony fought to keep control, a lost cause because she dropped to her knees and took him in her mouth. All he could do was moan as his fingers clutched at her hair, still tied up in that sexy upsweep.

Sweet gods of science. It didn't take her long to get him off, a few wet sucks and he bucked into her mouth, his hot cream spurting in record time to his embar-rassment.

He expected her to laugh at him, make some comment about his premature ejaculation and he prepared to flee with his shame. But truly, the woman was a goddess because instead, she said, "Been a while, huh?" He nodded, too humiliated to reply out loud. "Don't worry, now that we've gotten that out of the way, it's going to make round two all the better."

Anthony's eyes widened. *We're not done? I must be dreaming.*

She stood up and plucked his glasses from his face. "We wouldn't want to accidentally break these." She placed them on the small table by the door before she stepped back from him. Slender fingers reached up to her hair and released a clip, letting it tumble about her shoulders in a silken dark wave. She then unbuttoned her wine stained blouse, and flung it back to drape over the lamp by the bed. She revealed firm round breasts unfettered by a bra. Even his less than perfect eyesight couldn't miss how her nipples puckered and as he watched with a watering mouth, they shriveled even further.

"Suck them," she said huskily. "I want to feel your mouth on me."

His cock twitched back to life at her demand, a fact he'd have found fascinating and worthy of study any other time. He forwent taking notes on this amazing phenomenon to cover the few feet that separated them in a daze. He placed his hands on the taut skin of her waist and drew her body up. Electricity sizzled at the contact and she sucked in a breath, her startled eyes meeting his. She raised her hand and ran her fingers down his cheek, tracing his lips. She inserted one between his lips and he sucked it, enjoying the way her eyelids drooped and her body swayed towards him.

"Mmm," she moaned. "Do that to my tits."

He didn't need further urging. He'd have walked on fire at this point for her. He bent down until he could grasp one of her nipples with his mouth. He inhaled it slowly, each suck bringing more of her breast and nub into his mouth. She cried out in pleasure and gripped his hair with her hands, pulling him tighter against her. He switched breasts, paying the same attention to the other. She growled, a soft primal sound that should have sounded stupid, but instead, spurred him on. He bit down on her puckered berry and she mewled, her hips arching forward against him, the soft skin of her tummy butting against his already rigid cock.

"I want you to do that to my pussy," she purred pushing him away. She moved towards the bed and stopped at its foot. She undid the side zipper to her skirt and let the fabric drop to the floor.

Anthony almost joined it in a boneless puddle when he saw she wore no panties. He definitely swayed as she stood there clad only in nylons and garters. When her hands went to untie them he spoke in a gruff voice he didn't recognize. "Leave them on. Please."

He saw her body shudder in reaction to his words and his confidence soared. *This woman wants me.* Logic, sense and science had no meaning here, only a primitive lust like he'd never known.

He stripped his shirt off as he moved towards her, enjoying her look of surprise. She ran her hands over his toned upper body with wonder. "A big cock. A lickable chest. What else have you been hiding, my giant scientist?"

He answered her with a kiss, suddenly glad he spent an hour every day in the gym to keep himself fit—she didn't need to know that he used his mindless exercise time to puzzle out problems in the lab. She wrapped her arms around him and toppled them backwards onto the bed. He tried to brace himself so as to not crush her, but landed on her body anyway, not that she seemed to mind. Her legs wrapped around his waist, trapping his cock against her lower belly.

She kissed him, her lithe tongue sliding along his until he feared coming again, so erotically did she touch him. He pulled away, determined to give her pleasure. He embraced her body, worshipped it with his mouth and tongue as he slowly made his way down to her mound. He flicked his tongue against her still hard nipples and bit them just to hear that growling cry that sent a shiver through him. He laved a circle around her flat navel, fascinated by her toned physique, so different from his previous—if sparse—lovers. He caressed her body as he moved down to the neatly trimmed pubes and the treasure below. The proof of her desire glistened on her plump pink lips and he could even smell it. Her evident arousal awed him for he couldn't deny, nor could logic argue, this woman wanted him. It emboldened and enflamed him.

He knelt on the floor and grasped her thighs to draw her towards him, aligning her sweet sex with his mouth. Then he tasted her. At the first touch of his tongue against her pussy, she let out a keening cry and her back arched. He licked her again, a long wet swipe of his tongue between her lips up to her clit. She bucked and moaned.

"That's it, taste me. Suck me. Then fuck me."

Her crude demands fired him. He held onto her thighs and went to work, determined to pleasure her like she had him. It made his cock throb the way she trembled at his oral tease of her sex. He groaned at the way she tasted so sweet in his mouth. He flicked his tongue faster and faster over her swollen nub, her quickening cries goading him on. When her body tightened, he moved over her, sheathing his cock inside of her.

"Oh fuck," she growled, her low tone touching him in a primitive place that drove him wild. "Fuck me. Fuck me hard."

Anthony needed no urging. He pistoned his hips, thrusting himself in and out of her velvety moistness, holding back his release even as her pelvic muscles clamped him so tightly. He pumped harder, his hands on her waist, driving her down onto his cock. Deeper. Faster. Her fingers dug at his shoulders, her nails biting into his skin; the pain of it though, spurred him to plow her even more vigorously.

She screamed when she climaxed and her whole body bowed up off the bed. Anthony held on tight as her orgasm milked him in waves, and came seconds after her with a hoarse shout.

He collapsed beside her on the bed, breathing heavily, utterly blown away by the most extreme pleasure he'd ever experienced. She rolled against him, snuggling into him. He curled his arms around her, hugging her back.

"Spend the night with me," she whispered.

His answer of "Sure" sounded stupid and inadequate to him, but it seemed enough for her because her breathing evened out as she fell asleep.

I don't know how I got this lucky, but please, don't let it end.

Anthony was convinced he'd never fall asleep beside this goddess. In truth he feared doing so. *What if I wake and discover it was all a dream?* But, two orgasms in quick succession soon had him drifting into a pleasant dreamland where Lexie featured front and center—naked.

CHAPTER FIVE

LEXIE INCHED out from under her geek's arm, not because she wanted to—which surprised her and she'd analyze the why later—but because she heard stealthy movement from the room next door, the room her dear Anthony hadn't gone back to.

Getting him to stay with her—again part of her master plan to protect him—had gone off without a hitch and came with a fabulous orgasm. Who knew her unimposing scientist hid a gifted lover with a decent body and a large cock? While his pale skin seemed to indicate a life mostly spent indoors, his body had the general tone of a man who hit the gym daily, a fact she appreciated.

Later, she'd explore his body and his skills further. Time to earn her paycheck.

She briefly thought of getting dressed. Her nudity didn't bother her, and if the waiting assailants were male, it could give her the leverage needed. She did, however, grab her gun and Anthony's key card from his pants pocket. She glanced over at him and saw him still sleeping soundly. Hopefully, she could take care of the problem quickly and quietly before he woke. She peeked out through her peephole into the hall first.

Seeing nothing, not surprising give the time of three a.m., she opened her door on silent hinges and took the few steps over to the room beside hers. She decided against the adjoining room door because the time and noise needed to swing open the double barrier would have alerted them something was amiss. Better to let them think Anthony staggered back after a night of debauchery.

She slid Anthony's keycard into the electronic lock which disengaged with a snick. The motion inside the room halted as she'd expected. She swung the door open and sauntered in. Her nude body caught the waiting vamp by surprise, and he stared at her hungrily for only a moment before she shot him between the eyes. It wouldn't kill him, but it would incapacitate him long enough for the cleanup crew she'd call to take care of him.

Two more figures rushed at her from the darkness of the room and she shot another one before the third slammed into her.

The vamp tried to hug her, grope her and bite her all at the same time. Males, even dead ones, could be so predictable. She brought her knee up as hard as she could. The vampire folded with a pained gasp. She dropped to her knees and twisted his head until his neck snapped.

Round one taken care of and her geek safe for the moment, she made a quick call to Frederick's cleanup crew. All vampire families had one for situations like these that required discretion and, most of all, ensuring the humans remained oblivious.

She then sent a quick text to her employer mentioning the attempted poisoning at dinner—a plan foiled because of her sharp scenting skills. She also mentioned the nocturnal visitors and the fact his scientist now slept in her bed. Like he didn't know. She'd covered the lamp where the camera hid with her blouse, but their audio would have clearly picked up the sounds of their fucking.

Lexie slipped back into her room and crawled into bed with her giant geek. She still refused to examine why she smiled when, in repose, he threw his arm over her and drew her back into his body. She also ignored her wolf who whined in her mind, wanting something that Lexie didn't understand.

She buried everything that bothered her in the pleasure she roused by wiggling her bottom against his dormant cock. Lucky her, it didn't sleep for long.

CHAPTER SIX

ANTHONY WOKE ALONE. He sat up and looked around, but couldn't tell if this was his room or not. Hotels tended to lack imagination when it came to decorating. *Did I dream it all up?* Had he just passed out on his bed after he checked in?

The sound of running water came to him from behind the closed door of the bathroom and he looked about wildly for some clothes. Anthony didn't enjoy nudity, on him at any rate. However, he could have stared at Lexie naked all day long. But he was pretty sure she wouldn't feel the same way about him. Sure, he went to the gym and maintained a decent physique, but more for his general health than for looks. His pasty skin and hairless chest in the light of day weren't exactly his best attributes. He needed to cover up before she realized it too. He'd just found his glasses and snagged his pants when the bathroom door opened.

"Oh, goody, you're awake."

Anthony straightened, holding his pants to his chest and stared at Lexie as she sauntered from the bathroom wearing the tiniest towel imaginable. "Um, g-good morning," he managed to stammer. How this woman managed to make him sound like a simpleton, he still couldn't figure out. What happened to his calm and confident demeanor? His ability to analyze and respond appropriately to situations?

"It's a wonderful morning," she said with a smile. She approached him, her eyes glinting and he swallowed hard. "In the mood for some *breakfast*?"

A suave man would have said "Yes, now get your sexy ass on the bed so I can eat." Anthony just nodded his head.

"Excellent. I took the liberty of opening the doors between our rooms. I thought you might want to grab a shower and fresh change of clothes before we went down to eat. Then, I figured we could check out the conference events starting in an hour."

Anthony would have actually preferred pulling off her towel, throwing her on the bed and seeing if plowing her body really felt as good as he remembered. Instead, with a blush and his trousers clutched to his groin, he fled through the adjoining door, her husky laughter following him.

At least it wasn't the derisive kind he'd come to expect. He jumped into the shower, the hot water hitting his back and making him hiss. The sting of the scratches across his shoulders and upper back reminded him of her passionate response to their coitus. *She marked me.* The realization made him grin. As he showered his mind couldn't help turning over the fabulous turn of events that had occurred in the last twelve hours. He, proven geek and flop where woman were concerned, not only had a drop dead gorgeous woman seduce him—and suck him off—she still wanted to spend time with him. Even better, the sex had been amazing, the best he'd ever had, and more astonishing was her response to him. She hadn't faked her desire or her orgasm—he knew what a pulsing channel meant. And he suspected his middle of the night dream of taking her from behind while spooned in bed probably occurred as well.

Just thinking of her lithe body made him rock hard. He couldn't help gripping his cock and fisting it. He also couldn't help the low moan as he thought of the way he'd felt when she wrapped her lips around his shaft, sucking him while her hand cupped his balls.

The shower curtain rustled and his eyes shot open. Shock at getting caught masturbating made him want to swirl down the drain, until he saw her face. Lexie stood in front of him, the steam from the shower pearling on her skin, the expression on her face hungry, and not for food.

"I'm sorry," she murmured. "I just couldn't resist joining you." She wrapped her fingers around his hand still on his cock. "I hope you don't mind."

Anthony didn't mind when she bent over for him in the shower exposing the most perfect pink pussy. He didn't mind that the water made her tighter when he sheathed his cock into her. And he didn't mind at all that she screamed when he fucked her until they both came.

If his stomach would have stayed quiet, he would have suggested skipping the morning's events in favor of going back to bed, or the table, or wherever she preferred. However, he knew without some form of nutrition, no matter how his mind felt, his body would never keep up, and he was determined not to disappoint her. Even if the copious amount of sex with her made his dick raw, he had no intention of saying no.

CHAPTER SEVEN

LEXIE TRIED to pay attention to their surroundings and the possible threats to her geek sitting across from her, but dammit, she kept remembering how he'd taken her in the shower, which in turn made her so fucking horny. All she could think of was how fast she could get him somewhere private so she could screw his brains out again.

She didn't understand her insane reaction at all. Usually she got the itch, she fucked, and then she went on. Sure, this time she'd gone without scratching for longer than usual, but she'd gone through sexual dry spells in the past and never had a problem before. This out of control, raging desire to have this man in front of her—a geeky scientist and not her usual steroid body builder—baffled her. Sure he was cute in a nerdy kind of way. He sported a decent bod, nothing like her usual play toys whose abs could bounce quarters. His technique, while enjoyable—really, really enjoyable—was nothing new. So why, oh why, did she sit in drenched panties wondering if anyone would notice if she slipped under the table to give him a blowjob?

She must have stared at him for too long because he blushed and dropped his head. For a brilliant scientist, he took shyness to a new level, and she couldn't figure out why. After what they'd done together, she expected him to overcome his tongue tied demeanor. Or did he blush for another reason?

"Penny for your thoughts," she said. His color deepened and she smiled. No need for a penny, his face read like an open book. "If it's any consolation, I wish we were back in the room with my lips wrapped around your cock, too. But you came here for a reason, so I'm going to be a good girl, for now, and clamp my thighs tight and think of the lectures as foreplay."

He couldn't stifle the small moan which, in turn, made her squirm as more liquid heat seeped from her cleft.

Despite her good intentions—and the fact she wanted to have him out in public long enough to see if she could spot any more assassins/kidnappers—she couldn't stop fidgeting during the lecture given by the boring nerdazoid in the bow tie. She tried to focus on the speaker's words, but she couldn't help comparing the balding, short individual with her giant sitting next to her. She doubted she'd have wet panties had the dull, droning midget at the podium been her target.

She sighed as the lecture went on and on, absolute torture for an outdoorsy type like herself. Large fingers laced around hers and she darted a glance sideways to see Anthony with his lips in a half tilt. "What do you say we go for a walk? Somehow I think we'll learn more from the fresh air than this pompous idiot."

"Oh, thank god." She immediately stood, surprised at his initiative, but at the same time delighted.

They made it out to the vestibule and she wondered for a moment if their walk would take them back to her room—not that she minded. But Anthony, still on a take charge kick, strode with her towards the front door of the hotel.

"Where are we going?" she asked. She hadn't planned on leaving the building, and given her intimate relationship with her geek, not worn any weapons lest he find them and question their presence.

"There's a park one block over. I thought we'd go for a walk and then maybe hit an outdoor café for lunch?"

Lexie chewed her lip for half a second as she thought furiously. Given the bright sunlight, she wouldn't have to worry about vamps. The Fae and other creatures though, that could walk by day might see their excursion as an opportunity to move. The smart thing would have involved her plastering her mouth to his and convincing him to return to bed, but her animal side craved the fresh air and sunlight. She'd have to hope that Frederick's goons watched and followed. If she kept them to public areas where assassins would require subtlety if they attacked, she could handle the rest.

Her giant scientist kept a hold of her hand as they crossed the road and walked the short distance to the park. She found the intimacy of it odd. As a rule, she wasn't a hand holding, or cuddling for that matter, kind of girl. Her domineering presence and attitude tended to scare off a lot of men. Actually, if she weren't currently playing a role right now of cutesy science slut, she'd probably have sent Anthony running, too. It wasn't that she eschewed femininity, she just had a dominant persona that most men couldn't handle.

They reached the park without mishap; although, she kept her eyes peeled as she breathed deep of the air that wasn't entirely fresh given the exhaust of passing traffic. But it sure beat recycled hotel air.

"Do you spend a lot of time outdoors?" Anthony asked as they strolled along the cobbled path.

"You might say that." While she lived in the city during the week, on weekends and vacations she went to the woods where she ran wild and lived off the land.

"I love the outdoors." At her pointed look, he laughed, the most carefree sound she'd heard him make thus far. "I know. I've got the coloring of a lab rat. But, before I got caught up in my research, I used to spend a lot of time outdoors."

Lexie found herself listening attentively to the first freely given personal information from him. Where his sudden relaxation came from she didn't know, but she encouraged it. "Do you love the whole research thing?" she asked.

"It obsesses me. It's like having a puzzle with a few extra pieces and knowing if you can just figure out which one fits, you'll get the whole picture. But, enough about me. What do you do?" he asked peering down at her. "You never did say."

Lexie's prefabricated lie of working as a college professor's assistant got tossed aside in favor of a partial truth. "I do odd jobs for those who require finesse and subtlety."

"You know that doesn't tell me anything."

She grinned up at him. "I know. My jobs all have confidentiality agreements. Let's just say I'm good at what I do and well compensated, which, in turn, allows me a lot of freedom for things like this conference."

"I almost didn't come. I'm getting real close to a breakthrough on my current project. If it weren't for the fact my paper got selected, I would have probably stayed in my lab." He squeezed her fingers and smiled down at her. "I'm glad now I didn't."

Guilt stole her tongue and made her drop her eyes. She didn't understand it. She'd gotten her geek job right where she wanted him—eating from the palm of her hand and safe with her. But why did she want to beg his forgiveness for misleading him, and even worse, want him to keep looking at her with that smile in his eyes? *Don't get attached, Lexie. You know humans and werewolves can't be together,* not if she wanted him to live a long and healthy life. The reminder didn't cheer her.

CHAPTER EIGHT

ANTHONY CURSED himself for being an idiot. He'd spoken the truth about how happy he was to meet her and Lexie couldn't look him in the eye since then. She kept her hand laced in his though, so maybe all wasn't lost. *Idiot! Why not drop to one knee and declare undying love? Why not try a little harder to make her run by acting clingy?*

He blamed his runaway tongue on the insane feelings she roused in him. Lust yes, but more than that, she captivated him. He sensed some of her sweet girl routine was an act, hiding a woman who tended to dominate, a woman used to wielding power and having people around her obey. The fact she couldn't talk about her job intrigued him, and at the same time made his whirring mind wonder if she had an ulterior motive in befriending him. But he squashed that thought. She'd made no attempt to pump him for information, on the contrary, the only pumping involved mutual pleasure. He wanted to trust her interest in him was genuine, but he couldn't help a nagging fear that she wanted something from him.

When their walk turned silent as they passed through the woods, he found himself watching her. She looked everywhere in the miniature city forest, everywhere except at him. Watching out for possible muggers during daylight or avoiding him? He decided to see if lunch would rouse her. He led them out of the park and a moment later she relaxed and smiled up at him.

"So where are we going next?"

"You'll see," he replied enigmatically. He directed her to an outdoor bistro he'd noticed on his way in to the hotel. It offered a roof top patio with fabulous views which he hoped would make her forget his tacky declaration of earlier.

The elevator up with others forced her against him, not that he minded, especially when she slipped her arms around his waist. Of course, he could have done without the inevitable reaction of his cock and her knowing laugh.

The metal doors slid open and spilled them out onto a rooftop partially covered by a canopy. A hostess halted the group that crowded out in front of them. Anthony, seeing the many buzzing tables, worried that he hadn't made a reservation first, but luck remained with him. Although the large group ahead of them was forced to wait, the hostess quickly bustled them off to a secluded table for two around the back of the elevator. Screened with potted plants, Anthony could almost imagine he and Lexie were alone.

She broke the silence. "What a fantastic place! How did you find out about it?"

Anthony shrugged. "My employer mentioned it to me. Said if I happened to bump into a gorgeous woman, I should make the effort to take her here for dinner. He recommended I do it at night, but I thought you'd enjoy the sunshine more."

"You were so right." Her smile at him warmed him more than UV rays of a thousand suns, and he managed to bask in her pleasure without blushing for once.

The silence broken, the conversation flowed lightly as he made sure to stick to easy topics like the weather and movies.

Lunch passed uneventfully, unless he counted the way she kicked off her shoes and stroked a foot up his calf to settle it on his lap before rubbing him with it.

He was ready when she announced, with a vulgarity he enjoyed way too much, "Let's get out of here and fuck." He threw some bills down on the table and wished he could fly when the elevator took too long to arrive. By the time they reached her room, he was just about incoherent.

Sensing his need, she yanked up her skirt and bent over. He retained enough control to know he wouldn't last long enough to give her what she needed. He dropped to his knees and then just about came anyway at the sight of her soaked panties, proof of her own arousal.

He dragged her undies down and ran his hand over her cleft.

She growled, "Don't fucking tease me. Give me your cock, now!"

He obliged and to his surprise, she came first; although, he followed closely in second.

CHAPTER NINE

LEXIE STRAIGHTENED Anthony's tie instead of tearing it off. She ran her hands down his chest and his jacket smoothing it. "You look dashing," she declared.

His lips quirked into a smile. "If you say so. I don't think the audience will care. We science geeks tend to be more interested in facts and argument than clothes."

"And that's what sets you apart. You're head smart and dressed smart. I can't wait to see you in action, well, somewhere other than the bedroom that is. We both know you rock there already."

What only a day ago would have set him to blushing, now made his eyes twinkle behind his lenses. He kissed her, his shyness of before gone with the confidence he'd gained in her presence—she blamed her wet panties from lunch for that. If she'd found the shy geek cute before, she found this more self-assured side even sexier.

They went down to the conference area, splitting up

at the door as he went to the front to ensure everything was ready for his coming presentation. She took a seat in the back and carefully watched everyone who entered. They'd spent a quiet, attack-free day, and she didn't trust it at all. Two attempts on their first night and then nothing? She knew the best attempts were yet to come. She needed them to come so she could remind herself she was here for work and not pleasure. Despite all the men her mother had thrown at her, all the males who'd tried to claim her and the humans she'd toyed with, none had affected her like Anthony did. She still hadn't figured out why, nor did she intend to. Once she completed this job, she'd move on, like she always did.

As the time for Anthony's speech neared, the room began filling and she moved forward until she sat in the first row. Let Anthony think her eager, she wanted the proximity in case she needed to protect him. He glanced at her from time to time, not having forgotten her presence, and his quick smiles warmed her even as she chastised herself for acting so stupidly girly.

The lights in the room dimmed and the crowd hushed as Anthony stepped to the podium. She'd expected him to appear flustered, or hesitant, but when he spoke, she shivered. Apparently his shyness was reserved only for her. In front of his peers, the man was a genius and he knew it.

He spoke, and even though he used words she didn't quite understand at times, she found herself riveted for he spoke of her. Well, not her directly, but her species, werewolves, and not just shifters, but vampires and even the Fae, too.

The more he spoke, the more Lexie grasped just how dangerous her geek truly was. Not dangerous in a Rambo gun toting way, but even more lethal because his research was allowing him to unravel the truth of their existence. With his understanding of their DNA, he could possibly cure their state of supernaturalness, or even scarier, improve it.

Of course, he still believed the DNA he examined came from a human, a human with mutated genes. It was even possible his theory was true, that in fact, beings long thought special or paranormal were in truth a simple birth defect, a twisted DNA strand in the original human strain. It humbled and at the same time frightened her. She finally grasped just why so many factions might want him—dead or alive.

Holy fuck, what if he does find a way to twist the vampire strain in a way that makes them impervious to sunlight? What if he expands his research and discovers a way to make shifters invulnerable to silver, or strips the Fae of their powers? A lot of 'what ifs', but Lexie didn't doubt for a moment that Anthony would succeed. *He's just too smart for his own good.*

At the conclusion of his oration, the silence hung thick, then the questions came fast and furious from the nerds in the crowd who dared question his brilliance. Anthony handled them all with aloof aplomb. This was his element. He had the facts on his side and he used them against the naysayers.

Lexie didn't raise her hand, how could she when she was one of the monsters he considered still human, if special. *I wonder what he'd think if he knew the woman he was fucking turned hairy on the full moon or when I get really freaking pissed?*

But knowing how he'd turn from her in probable horror and disgust—or even worse, with a clinical eye towards experimentation—didn't stop her from wanting him. As the crowd thinned, she stood up and caught his eye. He broke off from the group around him and strode towards her, his face flushed with triumph. He grabbed her and kissed her, more forcefully than all his previous embraces. She melted under his touch.

He pulled back and smiled at her. "Come on. I'm starved."

So was she, but not for the five course meal being served. Nevertheless, she wouldn't take his moment of glory from him for selfish, sweaty sex. She did, however, make him a promise for later. She leaned up and whispered in his ear. "That was so fucking hot, and I'll show you later just how much it turned me on." Then she nipped his ear with her teeth.

CHAPTER TEN

ANTHONY ALMOST WENT CROSSED EYED at her words and his cock immediately went rock solid. Screw dinner, she was the only feast he wanted. *Now*.

He dragged her into the side chamber where they kept the presentation equipment stored. He kicked the door shut and shoved a chair under the handle.

When he turned back to face her, he saw her panting. She licked her lips as she watched him with bright eyes and flushed cheeks. She threw herself at him, her hands grasping at his hair as her hot tongue found the seam of his mouth and slipped in. Anthony groaned and clasped her tight to him, squeezing her perfect ass.

"God, you were so fucking hot up there," she panted.

"If you say so. The entire time I could only think of how I wanted you to spread those legs so I could see if you wore panties." His brazen words spilled from his mouth, but he forgot to get embarrassed when she grabbed his hand and guided it up her skirt. He touched her moist flesh and groaned.

"You are a goddess," he murmured as he rubbed his thumb against her clit. She clutched at his shoulders with a gasp and threw her head back.

The closet he'd dragged them into didn't exactly have a bed or open spot for him to take her. Although, it did have a bare section of wall. Anthony pushed her back against it and fumbled at the closure for his pants. Lexie helped him to unbuckle and shoved his pants and briefs down far enough for his cock to spring forth.

She'd grasped his plan and wrapped her arms around his neck as he palmed her ass cheeks. A little heavier than expected, he still hoisted her up and she aided him by wrapping her legs around his waist, drawing his cock into her moist pussy as she did so.

Anthony hissed at the feeling. He pressed her back against the wall and thrust into her. In and out, he claimed her sweet flesh, feeling her mounting excitement in the way her moist sex clamped his cock.

A rattle of the doorknob to the closet distracted him for a moment, but instead of shriveling his desire, knowing that people passed just outside the flimsy wall excited him. He plowed her faster and she urged him on.

"Oh, yes. Fuck me. Fuck me hard," she murmured squeezing him tight.

His fingers dug into her ass cheeks as he bounced her faster on his shaft. His balls drew tight under him as he slammed into her over and over. He feared getting too rough in his enthusiasm, but the harder he went at her, the wilder she grew. She must have remembered their public location at the last minute because instead of screaming like she did in their room, she leaned forward and sank her teeth into his shoulder.

Thank science for his jacket, which took the brunt, because she nipped him hard, but the pain mixed with the pleasure catapulted him into his own orgasm. He gasped as his knees trembled with the force of his climax, his hot cream jetting into her still quivering sex.

She unwound her legs from his waist and slid down with a contented sigh. "You just keep surprising me, don't you? And here I took you for a bedroom only type of guy."

Funny, that's what I thought too until I met you. And he loved it.

CHAPTER ELEVEN

THEY EMERGED from the closet furtively like teenagers afraid of getting caught; not that anyone remained in the conference hall when the bar was open and serving drinks next door along with a buffet.

On impulse, she twined her arms around Anthony's neck and kissed him. "Thanks."

"For what?" he asked.

"For showing me science can be passionate instead of boring." She recognized her error when his brow knitted. Her statement clashed with her first day claim of loving his paper in the journal. To distract him, she kissed him again and when she had him properly flustered, she dragged him out into the corridor where conference goers milled. They made their way hand in hand to the hall, where the buffet sat on a long train of white cloth covered tables. Some of the dweebs from Anthony's conference swarmed him, firing questions. Anthony answered them whilst squeezing her hand as if to remind her she wasn't forgotten. But Lexie had a more pressing problem and it was leaking down her legs.

She leaned up on tiptoe to murmur. "I need to go visit the bathroom. I'll be right back." She kissed the corner of his jaw and slipped away.

Lexie didn't like leaving him alone to go to the bathroom to deal with her sticky thighs, but surrounded by a herd of nerds, she figured him safe for the few minutes it would take her to clean up.

She did her business quickly, washing herself off with a silly grin at his impromptu act. Who'd have imagined he'd garner the nerve to haul her into an oversized closet and fuck her against a wall? She couldn't deny her corrupting influence in this case.

Crotch wiped down, hair brushed and her makeup repaired, she re-emerged into the hall, her eyes immediately zoning in on Anthony, his height a definite advantage among these odd looking trolls. Finding him safe, she scanned the hall for danger as she approached, but saw nothing, which didn't reassure her. When she got within fifteen feet, with her enhanced hearing, she caught the conversation swirling around Anthony and growled under her breath.

"So Savell, where did you go and hide last night? We kind of expected you to join the meet and greet or were you too chicken to hang out with real scientists?"

She saw Anthony's body tighten and she clenched her fist, not liking the tone of the taunt. "I was otherwise occupied," her scientist replied enigmatically.

The short nerd whose lecture she and Anthony had skipped out on sneered. "Oh, please. Admit it, you were afraid we'd rip you a new one and shred your theory to bits."

Lexie had heard enough. She slid up behind Anthony and wrapped her arms around his waist. "Hi sexy," she murmured. She nudged his arm and he raised it so she could slide around his body to press against his side. She smiled at the gaping nerd crew.

"Well hi there, boys. I do hope you'll forgive me taking up so much of Anthony's time. The man is a tiger in bed, and well..." She ran her hand up his chest. "I just hate to waste good hotel sex time."

Anthony coughed behind a hand and his body shook.

"Uh. Ah. Gee." The little geek who'd dared ambush her giant scientist blushed and stammered.

She turned into Anthony's arms with a pleased smile. "Let's dance, lover," she purred.

Only once they hit the makeshift dance floor did Anthony's shudders turn into laughter. She peeked up at him. "What's so funny?"

He grinned down at her, his smile so natural and filled with mirth it made her heart stutter. "Anyone ever tell you that you're amazing?"

"Shut up." Lexie ducked her head as her cheeks heated over his compliment. Blushing, a new thing for her, and she didn't like it one bit. It made her feel...vulnerable.

He chuckled and she rubbed her face against his chest, enjoying the rumbling sensation. They continued to dance in slow circles that allowed her to see in a three sixty angle if anyone looked out of place. In this room full of dweebs, geeks and nerds, the suave gentleman in the immaculate suit stood out like a sore thumb.

Lexie pulled back from Anthony. "I could use a drink, something sweet and nonalcoholic."

"Sure."

"I'll be standing by the exit door," she said pecking him on the lips. Or meant to. He crushed her to him, lifting her until she stood on tiptoe so he could thoroughly plunder her mouth.

With a cocky grin, he left her at the edge of the dance floor and made his way to the bar. Bolder and bolder, her geek job had not only grown a backbone around her, he'd also grown some balls. *How cute.*

Lexie pretended to wander aimlessly, but all the while she noted the thug in black. As expected, he went after the supposedly easier target—her.

She allowed him to grab her and bustle her out the exit door. Once outside she played innocent a while longer. "Wh-what do you want?" she cried, clasping her hands.

"I need to talk to your boyfriend."

"Anthony? Whatever for?"

He pulled a revolver out and pointed it at her. "Just do as I say and no one will get hurt."

Lexie dropped the fragile human routine and laughed. "Seriously, does that line ever work?"

The lackey's brow creased. "Shut up before I shoot you."

"Go ahead. It wouldn't be the first time." She didn't want to ruin her dress though, or her evening. She hiked her skirt drawing his eyes down to her legs and the foot that swung up to connect with his chin. The loud crack preceded the thug's eyes rolling back in his head. He sank to the ground in a slump and Lexie scoffed at the ease with which she'd taken him down.

Too fucking easy. Shit.

She scurried back inside in time to see Anthony with a puzzled brow being escorted out of the hall. She darted back out the side door and ran around to the front of the hotel. She skidded around the corner, glad she wore flats instead of heels, and quickly walked to the front doors. She slowed, smoothing her dress, and strode in just as Anthony and his expected captors appeared.

"Darling, there you are," she gushed. "I'm sorry I wasn't waiting for you by the door, but I got so hot, I just had to get a breath of fresh air." She could see the panic in his eyes and his not so subtle hint via head shake that she needed to go away. She wanted to kiss him for his attempt to protect her.

"Are these friends of yours?" she asked with wide eyed innocence. She stuck out her hand. "Hi, I'm Lexington, Anthony's girlfriend."

The goon on the left threw a puzzled look at his partner on the other side. With a shrug, he thrust his hand out grabbing hers, but when he squeezed and would have pulled her into him, probably as a hostage for Anthony's good behavior, Lexie returned the favor —harder.

THE GEEK JOB 59

"Lexie. Run," Anthony finally yelled. "They've got a gun."

"But that's illegal," she said still playing the part of innocent. She sensed movement behind her and thrust her elbow back connecting with a sickening crunch. "Oops. Sorry about that."

The click of a gun cocking made her sigh and she raised her hands as the barrel poked her in the back. The jig was up. She'd now have to kick some serious ass and as a consequence, probably forgo one last night of great sex because there was no way Anthony wouldn't clue in if he saw her take down these thugs without breaking a sweat. She coiled and prepared to unleash her nasty side as Anthony's face struggled through a myriad emotions—disbelief, fear for her and finally anger.

What her geek lacked in finesse, he made up for in size and adrenaline. He stomped down on the foot of the assailant holding him and then shoved him hard sideways. While Anthony was occupied, Lexie donkey kicked the idiot behind her catching him in the nuts. He crumpled and she flew into Anthony's arms.

"Oh, Anthony. Are you okay?" she asked, keeping his attention on her as hotel staff finally came running to deal with the commotion. Not that they did anything as the wanna-be kidnappers, with their cards played, fled out the door.

Anthony appeared dazed and looked around in confusion. "I—What—How?"

"We're safe. Those petty thieves are gone. You saved me." And she even managed to keep a straight face as she said it.

"I did?" The stunned look in his face made her want to smother him in kisses.

"Oh, yes, you did," she smiled. "Come on. Let's get out of here and go up to our room so I can properly thank you for being my hero."

"But shouldn't we call the police?"

"What's the point? We're fine. They're gone. Besides wouldn't you prefer to spend our last night naked in bed rather than in a boring police station?" She coaxed him. When the staff would have stopped them with questions, she pretended to faint. Anthony caught her slumping body and took charge. He swept her up into his arms.

"Sir, we need you to give a statement to the police."

"About what? Your gross incompetence where the safety of your guests is concerned?" Anthony sounded really pissed. "Thankfully, the miscreants where chased off with no help from this establishment. They didn't actually manage to steal anything, so what exactly would you like me to accuse them of? Showing how feeble your security truly is?" Lexie bit her tongue so as not to giggle as she imagined her geeky lover facing down the hotel staff. "Idiots. Get out of my way so I can get my girlfriend back up to our room."

Feigning unconsciousness, Lexie didn't know what she found sexier—his domineering manner with the hotel staff or the fact he called her his girlfriend. Both made her tingle all over.

He carried her into the elevator and punched the button for their floor. Once the doors closed, she nibbled his jawline.

"I thought you might be faking it."

She laughed. "I'm horny and they were getting annoying. Nice job getting us out of there."

"Care to tell me what happened?" he asked tilting his head to look down at her.

"What do you mean?"

"Those guys. They wanted to kidnap me, not rob me."

"Are you sure?"

Anthony sighed with exasperation. "I'm not that oblivious. Just like I know you did something to get them to let me go."

Lexie widened her eyes. "Me? I didn't do anything. You saved me."

Anthony narrowed his gaze. "Don't toy with me, Lexie. I might have taken care of the one thug, but you did something to the other one. And how did you know to come around to the front of the hotel to intercept us? Who are you?"

"Nobody."

He snorted.

Lexie sighed. "Fine. You caught me. Remember how I said I'm kind of an odd jobs kind of girl? Well, sometimes the things I do can get a little dangerous, so I've had to learn how to protect myself. When I came out of the bathroom and saw those thugs carting you off, I couldn't just do nothing. I couldn't make it through the crowd in time so I let myself out a side door and ran around to the front. I'll admit, I did act a little pretending to not grasp the situation, but I didn't want those guys to see me as a threat. When I grabbed the one fellow, I used some pressure points I learned to temporarily incapacitate him. But you took care of the other on your own," she reiterated pressing herself against him and slipping a hand down to cup the growing bulge at his groin.

"I did, didn't I?" His smile emerged, banishing his doubts for the moment. Lexie knew she'd squeaked by with her feeble explanation, and given time, when he'd thought it over more fully with that fabulous brain of his, he'd probably have more questions. So, she'd just have to make sure to keep his focus distracted until the limo showed up to take him away in the morning. She'd ply him with erotic pleasures to keep him occupied the rest of the night. *The things I do for my work—numerous orgasms and pleasure. What a way to end the job.*

They arrived at their floor and she took charge. She grabbed him by the tie and tugged him after her. "I've got a special reward for my hero, that is, if you want it?"

His lips quirked when he replied. "Depends. Are you going to use some of those pressure point moves on me?"

She used his tie to reel him into her and she stood on tiptoe to murmur against his mouth. "Oh, definitely. Did you know about the one on the head of your dick? It's guaranteed to bring you to your knees. Maybe I'll just show you with my tongue how deadly it is."

His eyes lost focus behind his lenses and she felt his body temperature rise. He didn't answer her with words, but he did use his mouth. He kissed her fiercely, pushing her back up against her door and Lexie returned his embrace as her hands fumbled to yank out her key card to unlock the door.

They staggered into the room, and Lexie kicked the door shut before she stepped back to look at him. He met her gaze boldly. His adrenaline over his aggressive act downstairs and his arousal submerged his shy side, not that she'd seen it much lately as his confidence with her grew. She yanked his tie off and looped it around her neck for later. She slid his jacket off his broad shoulders and, in her impatience, she gripped the linen of his shirt and pulled the material apart, popping his buttons. He sucked in a breath at her rough handling, but she knew by the tenting in the crotch of his slacks that he enjoyed it.

She raked her nails down his bared chest, pinching his nipples as she made her way down to his belt. She unbuckled him and then undid his pants. His black briefs barely covered his erection and she slid her hand down the front of them to grasp him. She made a sound of satisfaction, a cross between a growl and a rumbling purr that made him groan. She pushed him back towards the bed, tumbling him onto the mattress. Her wolf rode her hard, pushing for control and Lexie closed her eyes lest their glow give her away. She breathed deep, reasserting her control over her suddenly anxious beast.

She straddled his waist, her skirt riding up and pressing her moist pussy against his stomach, her cleft still pleasantly swollen from their earlier tryst. When he would have grabbed her, she growled again. Her control held on by a thread and she didn't trust herself not to hurt him if he touched her. She snagged his hands and exerting some of her strength, she pulled his arms above his head and using the tie she'd saved, tied them to the head board.

His body stilled and he regarded her with a touch of trepidation. She whipped his glasses off to get the full effect of his stare—and to blur his vision so that he wouldn't clearly see anything like, say, her not so human side which fought to come to the surface. Besides, he had the most beautiful blue eyes and she hated to see them trapped behind his ugly lenses.

She grasped his tied wrists and leaned down to brush her lips over his. "Don't worry my giant scientist. I am about to help you discover the joys of bondage along with a good dose of tease."

She leaned back from him and in one fluid movement, stripped her dress off, leaving her bare except for her garters which she knew he loved. Under his avid gaze, she cupped her breasts, rolling and pinching her nipples between her fingers.

"Are you trying to drive me insane?" he muttered.

Lexie smiled. "What? And waste your beautiful

brain? Never. But I'm going to make you come like you've never imagined. Eventually..."

She laughed at the way his breathing hitched and his eyes lost focus. She especially enjoyed the way his hard cock twitched behind her, pressing against her backside as if alive and seeking the moist core it longed for.

She raised herself and moved back, pushing his thighs apart to rest herself between them. Having Anthony at her mercy calmed her wolf somewhat, but a wildness to possess this man, to ensure he never forgot her took its place. *I'll ruin you for all other women.* She didn't examine why the thought of him with anyone else made her claws pop and a low rumble emerged from her throat.

She dragged the sharp points of her nails down his muscled thighs and his body tensed. But even better, his cock jerked. She leaned forward, her face hovering over his appendage while her hair tumbled to tickle his groin. She blew on him, soft warm breaths that made his dick strain. She didn't touch it though, not yet. She puffed up and down its length as her hands cupped his balls, kneading them between her fingers.

He groaned and his body tensed up on the bed.

"Tell me what you want me to do?" she whispered. Could she make her geek talk dirty to her?

"I—." He swallowed hard.

She blew on his tip and watched a drop pearl, waiting for her tongue. "Tell me, Anthony."

"S-Suck me."

She peered up at him and saw him looking down at

her. A sheen of sweat coated his face while a reddish hue heightened his cheeks. "Like this?" She took his swollen head into her mouth, the salty taste of him on her tongue, making her moan. She gave him a hard suck then let him go with a wet pop.

"Yesss," he hissed.

"I'll suck you, but is that all you want? Do you want to come in my mouth?"

"Yes. No. I want you to ride me. Suck me, then fuck me."

Lexie's body quivered as he mouthed the dirty words. They sounded so strange coming from his lips, but they excited her. With a mewl of pleasure, she went to work, her lips sliding down the length of his shaft, taking all of him down until her lips touched the root. His hips bucked, but she held on tight. She sucked him, her cheeks hollowing as she inhaled tightly. She slid her mouth back up his cock, swirling her tongue around his head, then she plunged right back down. He thrashed as she deep throated him, over and over. She kept her pace slow, methodical, knowing it would drive him crazy. The balls she kneaded drew tight and she let them go. She also released his cock with a wet sound and sat up to regard him.

He sat on the edge of bliss, right where she wanted him. Now for her turn before she took him over that abyss. She sidled up his body and held her mouth just above his. He strained to kiss her, but she kept out of reach, the slow tease and denial exciting her.

She moved again until she straddled his face, her

pussy hovering over his chin. He stuck his tongue out and managed to flick the very tip against her slit. Lexie shuddered.

She lowered herself an inch. He laved her again and she moaned. But, she had another plan in mind. She flipped herself so she faced back toward his cock. She crawled forward on her forearms, leaving her cunt over his face while bringing her own visage above his prick.

Sixty-nine: her favorite number and position. She dipped her head down as she lowered her pussy. *Let the oral pleasure begin.*

Anthony latched onto her sex eagerly, his tongue probing between her lips to stab at her core. Lexie keened around the cock in her mouth, using her concentration on sucking him to distract her from the fantastic things Anthony did to her clit. He swirled his tongue around it, then rubbed it before sucking it between his lips. She felt the moisture seeping from her, soaking him and coating his tongue. She didn't remember ever getting this aroused for anybody. Wanting someone so much she ached.

She'd initially planned to get off on his tongue and make him gush into her mouth, but she suddenly wanted to see his face as he came, imprint this special man into her psyche, a rainy day memory for the future.

She pulled her sex away, but he fought to keep her, his mouth tugging and giving one last suck to her pussy lips. She released his cock as well and turned back to face him, panting. She impaled herself on his shaft in one swift stroke unable to wait any longer. She cried out and he bucked under her, his tilting hips driving him even deeper. She closed her eyes at the ecstatic sensation, but opened them again once fully seated. He watched her with bright eyes and she shivered at the desire in them. *Why couldn't he be wolf so I could keep him?*

The astonishing thought made her lose control for a second and she found herself battling her wolf for supremacy. The bitch had lain in wait for a moment of weakness, but while Lexie sensed her she-wolf didn't mean harm to her geek, she didn't understand what she wanted.

Her hips began to move and Lexie, only partially in control, realized her wolf wanted to feel a part of this, to enjoy the pleasure found with this surprising man. Lexie closed her eyes knowing that even with his myopic eyesight that Anthony might find it odd that her eyes glowed. She rocked on top of his cock, the pressure on her clit making her channel squeeze the hard rod inside.

Faster and faster she moved, while the wildness grew in her. The urge to mark this male, to keep him, grew stronger and stronger.

A part of Lexie knew she should get off before she and her beast did something stupid and irreparable, but selfish pleasure won out, and she could only pray she wouldn't hurt him.

CHAPTER TWELVE

ANTHONY STARED UP AT LEXIE, her luscious body undulating on top of his, and realized something illogical and mind blowing. He loved this woman. He'd known her less than two days, but irrational as it seemed, emotionally and sexually driven as it was, he'd fallen for her. He wanted to say something, or at the very least clasp her to him, but with his arms tied, he could only buck under her as she used her pelvic muscles to clamp down on him tight.

Then he forgot what he'd wanted to announce because she opened her eyes and stared down at him, her usual green eyes changed somehow, and even more uncanny, they glowed. His mind refused to accept what he saw and he shut his eyes, blaming the change in her eyes on hotel lighting and on the fact he didn't wear his glasses. People's eyes did not reflect light like a nocturnal animal's.

Her hands came to rest flat on his chest, her sharp nails biting into his skin. She growled, a low sound that made his balls tighten. She buried her face in the curve where his neck met his shoulder and sucked at his skin as she continued to ride him. Anthony panted, trying to hold on for her, but she nipped him, her sharp teeth pinching his skin and he bellowed as his orgasm hit, shooting his seed deep inside her. The biting teeth squeezed harder and he winced at the pinching pain. She came with a shudder and a drawn out moan, the muscles of her channel flexing over and over, until Anthony, his dick so sensitized from her sensual play, thought he'd pass out from overload.

Her body collapsed on his, the tension of their love-making receding to leave her relaxed on him. Her warm breath tickled his skin and made up for some of the ache he felt from her bite. *She's certainly enthusiastic.* He didn't mind, although this level of roughness in the bedroom was new.

Her hands crept up and massaged his neck, pressing against his muscles. "I'm sorry," she whispered her face still buried in the crook of his shoulder. He meant to say for what, but his mind went blank.

Anthony woke hours later to find himself untied with Lexie snuggled into his side. *I can't believe I fell asleep on her like that.* He blamed it on the intense lovemaking they'd enjoyed. He stroked her hair, brushing it back from her face. So much mystery surrounded her. He knew she hid something from him, an important facet of herself. Yet despite that, he couldn't help wanting to be with her. She made him feel like...a man. And not just a man, but a virile one who could sweep a woman off her feet and also be her hero.

How strange for a geek who'd always dedicated himself to the sciences. Anthony hadn't even known he owned an ounce of courage until he'd seen her threatened by that thug. Funny, because when those same assailants ambushed him, he'd let them drag him out of there without a fight. However, when they threatened Lexie, fear for her safety triggered a sudden rage in him. In that moment, he'd acted, not caring for himself, just knowing he had to do something to save her, to rescue her from harm.

Great, I have hero potential, but I think the more important thing here is the fact someone wanted me in the first place. Mr. Thibodeaux always insisted on absolute secrecy and guarded the grounds which included the chateaux and his lab, with a vengeance. *And violently.* For a moment an image flashed of one of the nighttime guards, his chin dripping with blood. As quickly as he recalled the thought, it disappeared and Anthony crinkled his brow. What an odd thing for his mind to conjure, especially given he wasn't prone to watching horror or gore flicks.

Back to his previous problem—why would anyone want to kidnap him? And who? His project in Mr. Thibodeaux's lab, while exciting, was scoffed at by many in scientific circles. Could it be that someone other than his employer believed in and understood what he was about to accomplish? Anthony knew his research sat on a threshold that would possibly catapult him into the spot-light and worldwide recognition. If he looked at it from that angle, it made sense that someone other than his employer might want to steal that kind of knowledge and glory for themselves.

But surely, if he was in danger, Mr. Thibodeaux would have never let him leave, especially without a guard. Or had he.

Lexie stirred against him and Anthony stroked her hair pensively. Perhaps, had he spent more time out and about instead of making love to Lexie, he would have seen some familiar faces spread unobtrusively throughout the hotel, keeping an eye on Mr. Thibodeaux's investment.

His train of thoughts was broken by a hand that skimmed over his stomach and grabbed hold of his dick. "You're thinking too loud," she complained against the skin of his chest, before kissing it.

"Sorry. I was just thinking about the attack."

"I've got something better for you to do," she murmured, squeezing his cock.

A few minutes later, Anthony could barely remember his own name let alone what bothered him about the attack. Thankfully, he remembered her name and he shouted it as he came inside her velvety softness.

CHAPTER THIRTEEN

THE NEXT MORNING, Lexie packed as Anthony showered. The night had been chaotic with her making love to Anthony and then rendering him unconscious as she dealt with the factions trying to kill and/or kidnap him. She'd prevailed of course, but it pissed her off. *I'd kind of hoped we could just fuck like wild animals all night long.*

She'd managed a few pussy clenching rounds in between ass kicking, the final one occurring less than fifteen minutes ago while under the hot spray of the shower. At least while they were fucking, she didn't have to think of what she had to do next. She dreaded the imminent goodbye. Stupid, since she should have celebrated her fat bank account. The geek job hovered on the edge of completion, successfully so, so why did she wish Frederick would call and extend her use?

Just the fact she even thought of it made her lips

tighten. Anthony was simply a target that required protection and no matter the fun they'd had—and orgasms she'd enjoyed—he didn't belong in her life, and she didn't belong in his. Even if he could look past the fact she'd initially seduced him as part of her protection plan—a hard thing to overlook for any man with pride— her very heritage made it impossible for her to contemplate a future with him. Already, she had to fight her urge to love him more roughly. Hell, she'd almost lost it the night before and counted her lucky stars she'd only bruised him. Never before had she needed to fight her wolf like she did currently. Her inner bitch paced restlessly even now, urging her to bite and mark Anthony as if he were a shifter, a fucked up conundrum indeed. She needed to get away before she lost control and treated him like her body increasingly urged. Her violent brand of love was not something she recommended given his fragile human status. She'd maim him at the least, kill him at the worst.

The best thing she could do for him was walk away. Now, if she could only find the words to make him understand.

I am, of course, assuming he'll have an issue about us parting ways. Heck, for all I know, I was just a fun conference fuck. But she knew better. She saw how he watched her and came to life when she was near.

With a curse, she zipped her suitcase shut as Anthony strode out wearing just a towel around his hips while he used a smaller one to dry his hair.

"Thanks for letting me use your shower," he said

softly. "Weird how the plumbing in mine got all messed up. So, what's the plan?"

It was her turn to end up tongue tied. "Um, my cab is coming in about twenty minutes, so I need to get downstairs."

Anthony peeked at the clock. "Shoot, my boss's limo will be arriving in fifteen. I better get a move on. Wait for me, we'll go down together."

He dashed through the adjoining door and she heard the sounds of him rapidly packing, their last sweet love making session this morning having put them both behind schedule. The minutes to their departure crept by quickly, and it was in silence that they left their rooms with suitcases rolling behind them to the elevator.

Anthony wore what she liked to call his 'pensive face', his head slightly dropped as he tumbled a thought over in his mind. When the elevator doors closed behind them, on impulse she dropped her suitcase handle and pressed herself against him, her mouth seeking his hotly. He returned her embrace fiercely, his timidity of the first day, completely vanished.

The bell dinged and the doors slid open. Lexie broke off the kiss and grasped her suitcase before she stepped out. She immediately noticed Frederick's men—Lycans like her—waiting by the glass doors and her stomach plummeted. The geek job was officially over.

Her throat tight for some strange reason, she gave Anthony a smile that shone perhaps a tad too bright and managed a low, "Thanks for everything. Bye."

She turned and began to walk. Of course, escape wasn't that easy.

"I want to see you again."

Lexie froze mid step. Despite her half-baked theory this was just a weekend thing for him, she'd—hoped—expected this. With his simple statement, he dangled temptation before her, and for a moment she reacted; her body tingled in pleasure, her heart stuttered and her mind screamed 'Yes, I want to be with you, too'. Then reality intruded as she reminded herself, he was simply a job. Fun as the sex had been, they both had their lives to return to. He to his lab, and her to, well, doing whatever paid the bills in between full moons.

She turned back to face him, steeling her face and resolve. "I can't."

"Why not? I-I thought we had something going." His face showed bewilderment.

"The sex was great, thank you." Her cheeks warmed as did her pussy. "Very fun, but really, you can't tell me you expected this to continue beyond the conference? You've got your work you need to get back to and I've got a life, too."

She hated the hurt and confusion clouding his blue eyes, but he'd get over it. And once she got back to her home and day to day world, she would as well.

"But—"

"It was nice knowing you." She turned to walk away and, to her shock, her eyes brimmed wetly. However, tears and a strangely aching heart didn't prevent her from scenting the danger. She recognized the distinct odor of Fae.

She whirled back around screaming, "Duck." But her sweet geek regarded her with incomprehension, so she did the only thing possible. She dashed toward him, and when the Fae assassin stepped from behind the column in the lobby, she dove in front of Anthony whose eyes widened even as he still didn't recognize the danger.

The missile hit her upper chest, splitting open her flesh with barely a sound, but the arcing blood made up for it. The fiery touch of the projectile immediately sent her into convulsions. *Damned Fae and their poisons.* She hit the floor hard, not that she noticed, having already blacked out.

CHAPTER FOURTEEN

ANTHONY STARED in horror at Lexie's convulsing body, and his stomach roiled at the messy hole in her chest. Blood oozed from her wound, spreading in a deadly stain that spurred him into action. He dropped to his knees feeling helpless without his lab and equipment. He pressed his hands to her chest attempting to stop the gush. Around him he could hear shouting and the sound of return fire as his bodyguards, who'd waited by the front doors, finally sprang into action. *Too late.*

"Hold on, Lexie. I'll get you some help. Why the hell did you do that?" he cried. Anthony wasn't so oblivious that he'd failed to recognize she'd saved his life, taking a hit meant for him. He just didn't understand why, especially when she had no problem walking away from him in the first place.

If you didn't care, why throw yourself in front of me? Why? Tears blurred his vision as the hot liquid continued to seep sluggishly from her chest, staining his hands and cuffs.

Meaty hands grabbed his upper arms and lifted him. Anthony tore his eyes from Lexie to stare in incomprehension at the gorillas on either side of him, guards he recognized from the compound housing his research facility.

"What are you doing?" he yelled as they toted him out the hotel doors as if he weighed nothing.

"Bosses orders. We need to get you to safety," one replied, his cold eyes darting from side to side looking for signs of more danger.

"But we need to help her." Anthony tried to twist in their grasp, but they didn't relent and rushed him outside to toss him into a waiting limo. Anthony scrabbled to get out, but they slammed the door shut and the car took off with a lurch.

Anthony lost his temper, a rarity. "Stop this car right now. We've got to help her."

The dark gaze of his guard settled on him. "She's beyond our help."

A cold dread settled on him. "No. You can't mean— No, she's not dead."

But the grunt from his guard with the flat, "Sorry," hit him with the weight of a freight train.

Anthony sank in on himself, horrified he'd caused Lexie's death. Appalled that even though she didn't think enough of him to want to pursue a relationship, she'd obviously cared enough to risk and lose her life for him.

I am so unworthy. That thought followed him on the

car ride to the airport and during the flight on his employer's private jet back home. It dogged his footsteps as he dragged his ass up the stairs leading into the compound facility where the top floor served as a penthouse suite for him. It rang over and over in his mind as he ignored the flashing red button on his answering machine and didn't bother checking his email.

He stood with his shoulders slumped in the middle of his living room, lost and in pain. He raised his hands to rub them against his burning eyes, his tears having dried up hours ago. The rusty color staining his hands and cuffs made him gag as he finally noticed it. He stumbled into his bathroom and retched into his toilet. Once he'd emptied his stomach, his body heaved with harsh sobs. *Oh, Lexie.*

He showered, the dried blood caking his skin, running down the drain along with his tears. His bloody clothes he left on the floor, unable to deal with their disposal with his grief so raw. He tried to box away his emotions for a woman he'd known only two days. He attempted to not replay over and over her last heroic act. He wished he could forget, but Lexie had touched him in her brief stint in his life. *How can I forget the first woman who showed me what love was?*

He buried himself in his pillows, trying to erase the mental image of her death, but sleep refused to give him escape. He tossed and turned, his nightmares rehashing over and over those final moments. He couldn't help blaming himself and not just for the assassination attempt on him, which he didn't understand. He hated the fact he'd not told her how he felt, that he loved her. He lamented, even more, the fact that despite all his knowledge and brain power, all of it meant nothing when the need for action arrived. Helpless as a newborn, useless as a tit on a bull, he'd stood and watched as the woman he'd come to love saved his life, and as if that weren't emasculating enough, all his medical knowledge couldn't stop her from dying. He also cursed the guards who'd dragged him away, the ones who'd used their strength to force him from her side.

If only I were stronger or had that commanding presence like Mr. Thibodeaux, then maybe I could have saved her. Or at least, not let her die alone on the floor.

In the morning, things still appeared bleak. He wanted to do something, anything to remember the most amazing woman ever, but it appalled him to realize that he not only didn't have a picture, but he'd never even gotten her last name.

No wonder she thought it was just a fling. I never made much of an effort to get to know her. And now he had nothing. With that depressing thought, he dragged himself into the bathroom and noticed his bloody clothes lying on the floor. A light bulb went off. Blood meant DNA.

Anthony scooped up the stained clothing. He skipped his morning ablutions and breakfast and took the elevator down to his lab.

He flicked on the fluorescent lights and didn't pause to admire the vast space filled with state of the art equipment, all ridiculously expensive but needed for his DNA research. And now even more useful to get a DNA imprint, the only thing left of Lexie.

He separated flakes of her blood onto slides and deposited more into test tubes with various solutions. He ran her essence through a barrage of tests on autopilot. *Don't worry, Lexie. I'll find some way to keep part of you alive.*

CHAPTER FIFTEEN

LEXIE GROANED AS SHE WOKE. Her head pounded like she'd downed several bottles of tequila, something she'd sworn never to do after her last hangover when she woke up next to a buck toothed shifter. Along with the pulsing ache in her brain, her limbs felt weighted down. *What the hell did I do?*

Memory flooded back to her and she gasped. *Anthony!* Her eyes shot open to discover she lay in her own bed back in her house. And fuck did her chest hurt.

She lifted the covers and noted a bandage covering the area where the Fae bastard shot her. She peeled the tape and looked under. The skin appeared pink and tender, the violence of the wound taking longer to heal due to the use of poison. What a fucking pain, but still better than the alternative. Anthony and his frail human constitution would have never stood a chance. Speaking of whom, had he made it back to his lab safely? She'd never find out lying in bed.

She winced as she sat up, wondering how she'd made it from the hotel back home. A knock preceded a head peeking around the door.

With a sigh, Lexie leaned back onto her pillows as her mother approached with a tray of food. "Hi, Mom." Just her ill luck, her mother had come to tend her.

"About time you woke, Lexington. You had me a tad worried there." Her soft spoken mother arranged the tray on her lap and then perched herself on the edge of the bed.

"I'm fine, or I will be. Damned Fae," Lexie grumbled as she grabbed the piece of toast slathered in jam. "How long was I out?"

"Three days."

Lexie winced.

"I really wish you'd find a different line of work," her mother broached.

Lexie rolled her eyes. *Here we go.* "Mom, not this again. I'll have you know this last job netted me fifteen thousand in two days. Know of any other jobs that pay that well?"

Her mother's lips tightened into a flat line. "If you had a mate, then money wouldn't be an issue."

"Yes, well, I tried that and it hasn't worked out so well, has it?" One, she had issues kowtowing, and two, she had yet to meet a wolf she couldn't take down. If she was going to tie herself down for the rest of her life, then she'd prefer someone who could actually handle her. *Although, I didn't mind handling Anthony.*

She snapped out of her sudden daydream of her geeky scientist and realized her mother still spoke. "The only reason it doesn't work is because you refuse to act as a woman."

"Mom," Lexie growled in warning.

"Fine. But who's going to come and care for you when I'm not here anymore?"

Lexie didn't have an answer to that, so she kept quiet as her mother bustled around her room tidying up. She ate all the food and drank all the juice knowing anything less would have her mother haranguing her again. *What is it about my mother that makes her able to boss me around, no problem, but act like a submissive bitch around dad?* To give her dad credit, though, he did treat her mother like gold. What a shame more wolves weren't like him, or as big and tough. Even though he'd disowned her, Lexie still respected him, most of the time.

"I don't suppose you know if my target made it back safely?" Lexie tossed that out nonchalantly, but her mother whirled with wide eyes.

"Since when do you care about your targets after a job is done? If you ask me, that little human didn't deserve what you did for him. Unless..." Her mother's mouth open and shock spread across her face. "Don't tell me you care for that-that—"

"His name is Anthony, Mom. And no, I don't care for him, I was just curious if he made it back. No biggie." Lexie lied with a straight face, but her mother's lack of information made her heart flutter. She needed to find out if he was okay, but first she'd have to get rid of her mother before she had an apoplectic fit. "Mom, just forget I said anything. You know what I could really use is some ice cream. You know the cookie dough kind like you used to get me when I was little." Lexie truthfully hadn't eaten the stuff in about fifteen years, but her request worked like a charm.

"You must have run out because I didn't see any in your freezer. Why don't you just lie here, and I'll run down to the store and get some."

"Thanks, Mom." Lexie snuggled down in her blankets and closed her eyes, pretending to go back to sleep. She kept one ear cocked and tracking the movement of her mother as she gathered her purse and keys then went out the front door. Only when she heard the sound of her car driving away did Lexie dive out of her bed and go looking for her phone. With her mother the neat freak around, it took her a few minutes to find it stuffed in a drawer along with her gun.

Lexie grabbed both and returned to her room. She slid the revolver under her pillow and then scrolled through her phone book until she found the number she wanted.

She dialed and stared at the ceiling as she waited for an answer.

"Ah, so the she-wolf survives," Frederick Thibodeaux's smooth voice would have been sexy if he weren't so freaking dead.

"I'm not easy to kill. So listen, I don't recall anything

after that Fae bastard shot me. What happened?" In other words—had Anthony made it back safe and did he miss her?

"My incompetent guards let that Fae bastard slip through their fingers. They didn't live to regret it. Lucky for us, after you used your body as a shield, no further attempts were made on my scientist, and he's now back to work under my watchful eye."

"Oh. That's good." Relief infused her at the knowledge Anthony was safe. Now if only it would take care of her longing to see him again.

"Not really. You made quite the impression on Anthony. Since he thinks you died—"

"What!" Lexie yelled. "What do you mean he thinks I died?"

"What else would he think when he saw a hole blown in your chest? A human would have succumbed in minutes." Frederick replied matter-of-factly.

"You have a point," she grudgingly conceded. "And it's not like we'll see each other again."

"Don't be so sure. My enemies have grown bolder, and with my daytime guards executed for dereliction of duty, I find myself somewhat shorthanded."

Lexie wanted to scream, *I'll be there in half an hour,* but sanity prevailed. Much as she wanted to see him again—and her wolf paced in her mind eagerly at the thought—it was a bad idea on several levels. First, even if he got over the fact that she survived a deadly wound, he'd end up discovering their weekend tryst was nothing but a sham. Lexie wasn't sure she could handle his anger and condemnation. Although, on the other hand, perhaps it would help her to stop thinking of him. But then again, what if he forgave her and wanted to resume, did she have the will power to say no and even worse, how would she ever keep her wolf leashed? Even now, just knowing he missed her made her beast push at her control. What if she slipped and accidentally hurt him?

"Sorry, but I'm kind of busy." She blurted the words out quickly before she changed her mind.

"A shame. You would have been well compensated."

Lexie closed her eyes and gritted her teeth. "Well, thanks for the offer. Let me know if I can be of service again in the future." She hung up her phone and flopped back on her bed.

Anthony's okay. The geek job is over and I'm home. Time to forget him and his sexy blue eyes and get on with my life.

Thankfully her mother arrived with a huge container of ice cream to help with the healing process.

CHAPTER SIXTEEN

ONE WEEK LATER...

FREDERICK THIBODEAUX WATCHED with irritation as his once brilliant scientist sat with slumped shoulders in his lab, staring off into space, something he'd done in equal measures with moping, since he'd returned from the conference. Had the self-pity resulted in work getting done, Frederick wouldn't have cared. However, his resident geek had not managed more than a few minutes of work, so intent was he on his misery.

Unacceptable, especially with summer fast approaching. Frederick had walked in darkness for nigh on three hundred years and he'd grown damned tired of it. Anthony and his brilliant mind offered the first ray of non-burning light and hope since Frederick had succumbed to his curse. Frederick could handle the teeth, the pale skin, the hunger for blood, and even the hunt to feed, but he damned well missed the hot kiss of sunlight on his face. *And now, because that damned she-wolf blew him better than a practiced whore, my chance to day walk is shriveling faster than a cock in ice cold water.*

He'd tried to reassure Anthony that Lexie indeed lived, but his geek just turned disbelieving eyes to him and said no human body could have survived what she did. It occurred to Frederick to tell him that Lexie was as human as him, but somehow he expected that to meet with even more disbelief from his fact loving scientist.

It galled Frederick that he couldn't just mesmerize his pet geek, but playing with human minds was a dangerous endeavor, and a chance he just couldn't take.

Frederick growled and cursed—killed a few trespassers to blow off steam—but ultimately, he recognized there was only one solution to his dilemma and it arrived wearing skin tight leather on her sport bike. Frederick had to grudgingly admit her appeal. If he didn't treasure his life, or unlife as it was, he would have attempted to seduce her. However, life as a eunuch didn't appeal and wouldn't resolve his moping geek problem.

He'd chomped down on his pride and called Lexington for help. Initially she'd just hung up on him. Her brazenness made him see red and gave him a massive hard on. Defiant women were his weakness. Eventually, he got her on the phone and managed to spit out the terms for a new job. She agreed for a high price, higher than her previous demands because, as she'd told him on the phone, "Anthony's going to be pissed, and I'm really not into the drama." But at ten thousand a day, even she couldn't refuse.

Frederick drummed his fingers as he waited for his manservant to bring her to him. She arrived in his office, filling his space with the rich scent of her blood and a musky perfume. A lovely she-wolf indeed, and such a shame she'd probably rip his balls off if he told her. Haughty as she acted, Frederick had to restrain a snicker because regardless of her thoughts on him, she'd actually made him come quite a few times. While she'd covered the camera in the hotel room, thus denying him a view of her naked body, he'd enjoyed himself grandly, listening to the sounds of her fucking Anthony. He'd never expected her to be a screamer and he'd shafted his cock numerous times to the exquisite music of her orgasms.

Lexington paid him no mind and strode over to his screens, staring down with a tight expression at Anthony, slumped on a stool. "This is such a bad idea," she murmured.

"Well, maybe next time I ask you to play the part of temporary girlfriend you could do so a little less enthusiastically," Frederick replied dryly. "The man is crushed by your loss." And if he wasn't mistaken, the she-wolf appeared affected as well. How unexpected.

"Let's get a few things straight about this new job. I am here to protect Anthony this time, not fuck him. So you can forget about the naked entertainment. With the full moon fast approaching, be reminded that I will require red meat for both lunch and dinner, or I might start chewing on your staff. Also, you'll need to have Anthony put under lockdown starting at six p.m. the day of the full moon as I won't be of any use until the following morning."

"I've already spoken with the chef and he's put in an order for a few cows, so feeding you won't be an issue. As for the full moon, I've got a special code already in place that will automatically shut the place down tighter than a nun's thighs."

"Do you ever take anything seriously?" she asked in an exasperated tone.

"Very, but I've lived a long time and find humor helps pass the time. Now, please follow me if you will, so we can get you started. After all, there's no time like the present to reunite lovers and watch the fireworks."

Lexie growled and Frederick chuckled. Emotions would definitely run high in the next few moments, but it beat the depressing pallor of the past week.

Frederick led the way through his chateaux and underground tunnels to the building housing the lab and Anthony's apartments. He didn't warn his scientist of their impending arrival, preferring instead to surprise him. The human had a strong, healthy heart. He could stand the shock of seeing his dead lover come back to life.

Lexington strode alongside him, her body tense. Frederick could sense both anticipation and trepidation rolling off her. What a pity his feeding involved blood and not emotions like the psychic vampires who fed off extreme feelings. But even if it wouldn't feed his dark hunger, he'd greatly enjoy the live action drama.

He pressed his hand against console after console, each allowing them access deeper into the building.

"Quite the setup you've got," she remarked.

"Worth every penny if Anthony manages to reverse the curse of sunlight."

"Funny, I would have thought that not having to eat people for lunch and dinner would have been a higher priority." She threw him a questioning glance.

Frederick shrugged. "While eating from the source is more satisfying and fresh, blood is easily obtained, both the real and synthetic version. How much of a monster I choose to be is completely up to me. The sunlight factor, however, is deadly. Even the tiniest sliver of skin exposed to that brilliant beauty is enough to turn me into a puddle of steaming goo."

Lexington shuddered. "Okay, I see your point. I still say, though, that Anthony knowing what you are, a real vampire, would help him. How can he fully understand what he's curing otherwise?"

Frederick clasped his hands behind his back as he walked the length of the last corridor before the lab. "I'm beginning to believe you might be correct. However, it is not something I can just dump on him. His fragile human psyche couldn't handle it."

"I think he's stronger than you give him credit for."

"And that is why you are going to tell him you are a werewolf?" Frederick stopped in front of the door and faced her with an arched brow.

The she-wolf, who feared nothing, actually fidgeted and dropped her gaze. "Yeah, well, no. I hadn't actually planned to do that." At Frederick's chuckle, her chin shot up and she attempted to defend her position. "I mean, it's not like he needs to know what I am to fix me."

"But he will need to know if you are to become a couple."

Lexington scowled at him. "We are not going to be a couple. Humans and wolves, while they can play, do not stay together."

Frederick shrugged. "If you say so. But just so you know, if you do break him by accident, I could always turn him. He wouldn't be wolf, but he'd be strong and able to heal."

"Don't you dare," she growled.

Frederick flashed her a grin replete with fangs, then smacked his hand on the console which slid the door open and forestalled her rebuttal.

Anthony didn't even turn to see who'd arrived. He sat hunched on a stool, staring at a screen full of squiggly lines.

"How's the work coming?" Frederick asked moving to stand beside him while Lexington hovered by the door.

Anthony shrugged.

Frederick peered at the screen and pretended he didn't know what he saw. "Whose DNA is that?"

"It was supposed to be Lexie's, but I must have contaminated the sample somehow because it keeps coming up twined with a secondary strand."

"Forget staring at a screen. Try turning around and saying hello to the real thing instead."

"What?" Anthony lifted his head as Frederick spun the stool.

Then he had to catch his resident geek as he fell off it in a dead faint.

CHAPTER SEVENTEEN

"YOU ASSHOLE." Lexie swore as she knelt down beside her prone geek.

"What? You had a better way of announcing you'd come to visit from the dead?" Frederick drawled, leaning back against the stainless steel counter. "Why not kiss him and see if he awakes like a true sleeping beauty."

"Just get out and let me take care of this."

"By all means. Feel free to do so naked. I would dearly love a video to go with my soundtrack." Frederick chuckled as he walked away, then cursed as she tripped him and he smashed to the floor. "Evil bitch."

"Dead dick walking," she retorted. She ignored the leaving vampire as Anthony stirred, his eyes blinking behind his large lenses. She knew when he saw her because they widened and he sucked in a breath.

"Lexie?" He reached a hand up to touch her face and she couldn't stop herself from leaning into his touch. He sat up and before she knew it, he'd pulled her to him and latched his mouth to hers. Startled, she didn't immediately pull away, and that gave him a chance to ignite the heat she remembered all too well. Moisture pooled in her cleft, her nipples tightened and when he groaned against her mouth, she almost threw him on the floor to ravage and mark him.

With a soft cry, she broke the embrace and stood to move away. She heard the sound of him getting to his feet, then approaching. When he would have touched her, she sidled sideways, but turned to face him.

"Hello, Anthony."

"You're alive? But how? And shouldn't you still be in bed? What stupid hospital released you already?"

He fired questions at her and she took a steadying breath to feed him the lie she'd concocted. "It wasn't as bad as it looked." Feeble, but the best liars knew to keep it simple and to the point.

His brow creased. "Not as bad as it looked? You had a hole in your freaking chest!"

Lexie shrugged. "Not the first one, either. I heal fast. What can I say?"

She could see a storm of questions in his eyes, but given her pat answers, he bit them back in favor of, "Why are you here? How did you find me?"

Finally, the moment of truth had arrived, in one respect anyway. "Frederick called me."

"My employer? But how did he know where to find you?"

"I do odd jobs for Frederick." She could see the

confusion on his face as his mind and heart refused to put the obvious together. She gritted her teeth as she spelled it out. "I work for your boss. I just recently completed a job for him as a matter of fact." She couldn't mistake the moment all the pieces fell into place—his face tightened and his blue eyes turned arctic cold.

"You were paid to be with me," he spat.

"Paid to protect you, which I did," she amended, her voice husky as she fought the choking tears at his obvious anger. She didn't understand her reaction. Why did she care if the truth upset him?

"Paid to be a whore," he yelled.

"If needed," she cried back. "My primary objective though was to keep you safe, which I did in case you've forgotten. The rest ended up being a bonus."

He gaped at her. "A bonus? You used me. You made me believe you cared for me."

"No, I never led you to believe the weekend was anything other than two people having mutual fun." The fact she'd grown to care for him had been an unexpected snarl, but she kept that to herself.

"I don't believe this. Did you have a good laugh about the easy geek when you got home?"

"I was a little too busy trying to recuperate from getting shot," she snarled. "And for your information, I would never have laughed at what we did. I didn't fake those orgasms, or were you too caught up in your own pleasure to notice?"

Anthony moved to stand behind a counter, his hands

fiddling with the equipment there. "Fine. You enjoyed it. I enjoyed it. You survived and got paid. What are you doing here now?"

"Frederick is concerned for your safety. He's hired me to act as one of your bodyguards, seeing as how some of the others had to be let go."

"No." Anthony said the word flatly and refused to look at her.

"You don't have a choice."

He swung his head up and his gaze froze her. "Why are you doing this? Are you enjoying torturing me? Just this morning, I thought the wonderful woman I'd grown to care about had died. And then she shows up, very much alive and I find out everything I thought and felt was a lie."

"I do care for you, Anthony."

"Shut up. I don't want to hear your pity for the nerd who fell for your act."

Tears brimmed in her eyes. "I didn't mean to hurt you. And of all the things I felt and still feel for you, pity was never one of them."

Anthony snorted and dropped his head again.

Lexie stood, indecision swamping her. He'd made it clear, he didn't want her around, but Frederick seemed very concerned about his safety. Sure, she could step aside like Anthony wanted and let someone else take her place guarding him. However, no one would guard him as well as her, and given how much he hated her now, she wouldn't have to worry about hurting him with her brand of affection. Much as her wolf howled in her mind, and despite the ache in her heart, his rejection of her was for the best, the safest thing for him.

God, I hate it when I don't even believe the lies I tell myself.

CHAPTER EIGHTEEN

ANTHONY'S HANDS trembled as he tried to come to grips with the torrent of emotions swamping him. Anger at her subterfuge and a rare loss of control made him want to hurt her. She'd made him think she liked him, but she'd lied and played him for a fool. He'd fallen for an act. His eyes burned at the shame of knowing she'd never found him attractive, that she'd seduced him as part of her plan to protect him. *How could I ever have believed she did?* But even knowing she'd fucked him because she'd been paid, he couldn't forget she'd almost died saving him. A part of him even dared believe that while she'd beguiled him as part of her agenda, she'd enjoyed their lovemaking, make that their fucking. *Love was never involved.*

As if those emotions weren't enough to deal with, relief that she'd survived also invaded him. He'd suffered thinking she'd died because of him. Despite her treachery, it made him glad to know she lived.

Anger at her actions, relief at her survival, he could handle, but it was the last emotion that flabbergasted him the most and embarrassed him. Even now, knowing he'd meant nothing to her, his cock still wanted a piece of her. His whole body did, and he found that unacceptable.

"You need to leave." He pushed his glasses back up on his nose before raising his head to face her, trying to keep his expression placid.

She chewed her lip and didn't immediately answer. In that moment, Anthony finally really looked at her, the shock of seeing her return from the dead and the truths imparted now settling. What he saw made his erection thicker. Gone was the woman in sexy business suits and hot cocktail dresses. Vanished was the seductress in garters with a naughty smile. Facing him now was a babe dressed in skintight leather pants that molded her round hips. She wore an unzipped, waist length leather jacket, open just enough to reveal the low cut, snug fitting tank top that outlined her breasts and clearly displayed her erect nipples. Anthony swallowed hard, even more attracted to her now in her bad girl getup than before.

"I'm sorry my presence is pissing you off, but you're in danger. If you want to live, you'll suck it up and let me do my job."

Anthony closed his eyes and counted to ten trying to rein in his temper. Her words, though, had the effect of dousing his libido. "Whatever. You know what? I don't care. Just stay out of my way." He pretended not to see the hurt in her eyes. *What does she have to feel hurt about? I'm the one she played for a fool.*

"I'll be just outside the door if you need me." She turned, displaying a perfect ass encased in leather, and Anthony's resolve almost crumbled. Thankfully she left, the door sliding shut behind her.

"Fuck!" Anthony grabbed a glass beaker and whirled, throwing it at a wall covered in writing. It smashed, the glass shards flying while the liquid rolled in heavy lines down the wall. Chest heaving, he stared at the mess and wondered when his well-ordered, fulfilling life had gotten so messed up. Even odder, how had he allowed it? *There's a reason I love science. It never disappoints me.*

He dropped his gaze and focused on the screen displaying the genome results which made no sense. The twirling 3-D image mocked him and intrigued him because he'd never seen anything quite like it, never even imagined it was possible. He'd run the DNA sequence on Lexie's blood several times now, and each time it ended up the same. Two strands of different codes wrapped around each other in a complex double helix that fascinated him and actually stirred his brain with an idea that might work with his dilemma concerning Mr. Thibodeaux's genetic makeup. Tapping a few keys, he ran a sub routine to separate the strands and then run them through his database for comparison.

He wondered if Lexie would give him another sample of blood so he could see if the anomaly persisted or prove a simple contamination was to blame. Somehow he doubted she'd just roll up her sleeve for him to plunge a needle in the name of science. Although, there were other ways of getting DNA...

If she intended to stick around—an idea that excited him more than he liked or wanted to admit— then she was sure to leave traces of her passage in the form of hair, or even saliva. He preferred working with blood, but his curiosity didn't care at this point. Alive in body and mind, an invigorating feeling after the previous days in his catatonic state, he attacked his work with an eagerness he didn't examine. *It has nothing to do with her and everything to do with this discovery.* Or so he tried to convince himself.

While the computer ran the analysis on Lexie's DNA strand, he pulled up his genetic files on Mr. Thibodeaux, whom Lexie familiarly called Frederick. Just how close was she to his employer? Anger flared in him and he didn't understand its source. Why should he care if Lexie and his boss knew each other intimately? His hand clenched tightly around his pen and it snapped under the pressure.

Sweet gods of science, don't tell me I'm jealous? But he knew no other explanation for his extreme dislike at the thought of Lexie with his employer, or any other male for that matter. It seemed even though his mind wanted nothing to do with the deceitful woman, his subconscious and his body weren't quite ready to let go.

A yawn crept up on him and he peered at his watch realizing the late hour. He'd gotten used to starting his work later so his boss could come speak to him, his sun allergy keeping him out of sight until sun down. But

Anthony, while willing to compromise, still couldn't work wholly at night. He needed sunlight even if he didn't always get a chance to enjoy its warm embrace.

Leaving his machines running simulations that would take hours to compile, he made his way to the door only remembering as he opened it that Lexie waited on the other side.

She lifted her head as he appeared. Without a word, her face an indecipherable mask, she straightened herself from the wall she leaned against. A twinge of guilt suffused him as he realized he'd left her waiting out in the corridor without even a chair to sit in, but she said not one word of recrimination.

"I'm going to bed now," he announced, then his cheeks heated as he realized how it sounded. "Um, so I guess I'll see you tomorrow."

Lexie smirked. "Lead the way. As your new body-guard, you're not allowed out of my sight."

"I assure you this building is quite safe."

"No, it's not. It's decent, I'll grant you, but to someone like me, still too easy to infiltrate."

Anthony held his tongue at her statement. *What does she mean when she says "someone like me?" Just what is she capable of?* Deciding an argument would get him nowhere, Anthony led the way with his lab coat flapping, much too conscious of the fact she followed. He pressed his palm on the scanner for the elevator and the doors slid open.

"I'll have to look into getting added to this system," she mused.

"I can do it for you," he offered.

She turned amused green eyes toward him. "Yes, you can do it for me," she purred. She laughed when his face heated even hotter.

He didn't understand her game. Why flirt with him anymore? He was glad when the elevator arrived at the penthouse, the close proximity of the cab making him too aware of her, the subtle scent of her perfume wrapping around him and firing up his senses. He walked into his apartment and whirled to say good night, but she stalked around him, scanning the room.

"What are you doing?"

She didn't turn to face him when she answered. "Checking for danger, of course." She flowed through his space, her body moving with a fluid grace that dried his mouth. She looked like a dark predator in her leather, moving from room to room, her eyes scanning every nook and cranny, and even stranger, he could have sworn she inhaled the air, as if tasting it. The whole thing disturbed him even as it raised his body temperature and cock.

She finished in his bedroom and whirled to face him, because like a stupid puppy, he couldn't help following her. "All clear."

"Thanks, I guess. See you in the morning."

"Night." She flopped into the armchair by his bed and closed her eyes.

He watched her, puzzled. "Eh, what are you doing?"

She opened one eye and peered at him. "Guarding you, of course." She closed her lid again and Anthony ogled her.

"Can't you guard me from another room? I need to get undressed and go to bed."

Lexie sighed and forgot feigning sleep to regard him. "How am I supposed to guard you if I'm not with you? It only takes seconds for an assailant to kill you. Now stop protesting and do what you have to so we can both get some sleep."

Anthony gritted his teeth as he grabbed a pair of track pants and headed into the bathroom. No way was he undressing in front of her and making a spectacle of himself. He stripped in the bathroom and stared at his hard dick. Regardless of his thoughts on the matter, his cock appeared more than happy to have her stay.

Unwilling to embarrass himself further by walking out with a stiff prick, Anthony turned the shower on and jumped in. He stood under the hot spray and let it pound against his skin, relaxing his muscles, well, all except the rock hard one. He knew of only one solution to that dilemma.

He wrapped a soapy hand around it and fisted it back and forth. He tried to picture anything but Lexie as he pleasured himself; however, nothing in his past could compare to the ecstasy he'd enjoyed with her. His breathing hitched as he recalled a previous shower where she'd bent over for him, her round ass perfectly tilted to display her pink cleft. She'd watched him over her shoulder, her eyes heavy with passion as he slid into her, the tight walls of her channel clamping down on him. She'd come before him, the ripples of her climax triggering his, and now, like in the memory, as he stroked himself, he came again.

His body shuddered with minor aftershocks as the water washed away the traces of his climax, nothing like the quakes that rocked him when Lexie made him come in the flesh. He finished washing himself, trying once again to block her from his mind and thought he was doing a great job until he stepped out into his bedroom wearing a t-shirt and sleep pants and saw her splayed in the chair.

She'd kicked off her boots and let down her hair which framed her in a dark silken fall. She'd also removed her jacket, leaving her clad in her leather pants, which had to be uncomfortable, and a tight top that delineated her bust to perfection. His cock twitched and he almost ran to his bed to hide under the covers.

He tossed and turned in the large bed, unable to sleep knowing how wretched her current location was. He opened his eyes and looked over at her. As if sensing his stare, she opened her eyes and stared back.

"Is everything okay?" she asked.

"Yes." He sighed. "No."

"What's wrong?"

"I can't let you sleep in the chair."

Her gaze narrowed. "I already told you, I'm not leaving."

"I got that part. This bed is huge. It would be selfish of me not to share it."

Her lips twitched. "Why, Anthony, I never thought you'd have the nerve to ask."

He blushed at her innuendo. "That's not what I was implying. I wasn't asking for sex. I just can't in good conscience let you sleep in the chair when this bed has more than enough space for both of us. And, if you need something less confining to wear, I've got some shorts and track pants in the top drawer of my dresser."

"Thanks. I think I'll take you up on the offer. Frederick's goons apparently didn't bring my shit up." She moved to rummage through his drawer pulling out a pair of his jogging shorts, then, instead of going into the bathroom to change, her hands went to the button of her pants. Anthony shut his eyes and turned his head as she yanked her leather bottoms down, her amused chuckles making him heat and not just in the face.

He rolled himself over to his edge as she climbed into the bed. He held his body stiffly and he heard her sigh. "Good night, Anthony. Don't worry, I promise not to bite."

She said the words as if disappointed, and truthfully, Anthony was too. He'd quite enjoyed the way she'd nibbled him in the past. But as his mind reminded him, *she needed to get paid to fuck the geek.*

Holding onto his anger—and hurt—he fell asleep.

CHAPTER NINETEEN

LEXIE WOKE to find herself plastered to Anthony with an arm and a leg thrown over him. She immediately scooted away, appalled at her lack of control. She didn't allow the excuse of slumber to placate her. She couldn't allow herself to get involved with him, especially not this close to the full moon. Her wolf roiled restlessly in her mind and her pussy throbbed, the pair of them arguing against her plan of action, or in this case, inaction.

Too bad. Anthony is a human and deserves better than me. She used the bathroom while he slept, leaving the bathroom door open so she could hear if anything untoward happened. She quickly peed, showered and brushed her teeth with a spare toothbrush she found in the vanity. When she emerged, the bed lay empty with her geek nowhere in sight. Dressed only in her tank top and panties having forgotten her pants by the bed, she dashed out into the main apartment, sniffing the air and locating him along with coffee. She stalked into the kitchen, bristling.

"Don't you ever sneak off on me again," she growled, chastising herself for taking too long in the bathroom.

Anthony, already dressed for the day in chino's, a white shirt and a fresh lab coat, arched a brow as he held out a mug of coffee. "Good morning to you, too. Are you always this grumpy in the morning?" As soon as he said it, she could see him recall their previous mornings together where they'd woken in a more intimate fashion wearing smiles of pleasure.

She couldn't resist teasing. Why not, she already knew she was going to hell when she died. "I prefer your previous method of wake up involving hot sausage."

He flushed and he turned around to busy himself, but not before she caught his pants tenting. *I'm playing with fire. Good thing I heal quickly.* She sat down and watched him, unable to stop herself. It took him a few minutes, but eventually he turned around again holding two plates and his composure. He slid a plate in front of her before sitting down.

She grimaced at the scrambled eggs and microwaved bacon. "Are you trying to kill me?"

Anthony, seated across from her, regarded his own plate with a frown. "My cooking skills don't extend to the kitchen, but ask me to whip something up in the lab and I'm your man."

"Oh, I'd say the lab isn't the only place you can cook." Lexie wanted to slap herself as once again she flirted with him, but it wasn't entirely her fault. She got a kick out of seeing him flustered, and it didn't hurt her pride either to know that despite what she'd done, he still couldn't help desiring her.

Bad wolf. Stop baiting the human. Lexie couldn't wait until the full moon came and went so she could put her wolf to sleep. This close to the forced change, her wolf sat too close to the surface, just waiting for a chance to take over. *Not happening, my inner bitch, so settle your furry ass down. Anthony is off limits.*

Lexie choked down the breakfast using her coffee to wash it down. Thank god, she'd requested red meat for lunch and dinner. She'd starve if she had to rely on Anthony for sustenance, well, other than the wiener type.

Appalled that she couldn't keep her mind out of the gutter, she stood and didn't remember her lack of pants until she noticed Anthony's gaze riveted on her crotch, and of course, said crotch immediately got wet.

"I'd better finish getting dressed," she mumbled turning to leave. As she walked back to the bedroom her keen hearing caught the sound of him groaning and a thump as if he'd banged his head on the table. She couldn't help the smile that tilted her lips.

She slipped her pants back on, making a mental note to herself to find out where the hell her bag with her change of clothing had gone. Her shower had refreshed her, but without clean underwear, she felt scummy.

She jammed her feet into her boots and grabbed her jacket. Then she retrieved her revolver from under the pillow and slid it in the special holster inside her jacket.

She also patted her pants and coat sleeves to check that her silver blades were present. It never paid to go to work unprepared.

She returned to the main living area to find Anthony standing by the large floor to ceiling window. She cursed under her breath.

"Do you have a death wish?" she barked.

He turned with a puzzled frown.

"The window? Like, hello, would you like to paint a larger target on yourself for any snipers that might be outdoors?"

He gaped at her for a moment, then her geek found the nerve to laugh.

"This isn't funny, Anthony," she growled.

He snorted. "Yes, it is. I mean, seriously, snipers? First off, Mr. Thibodeaux has excellent security, and second, these windows are bullet proof. Apparently, you aren't the only paranoid one around here.

"Laugh all you want, my giant geek, but bullet proof glass doesn't stop everything." That shut him up and she slapped her hand on the console to call the elevator.

"You need to be put into the system for it to work..." He trailed off as the light turned green and the door opened.

Lexie bared her teeth in a smile that made him flinch. "You might be good at what you do, but I'm wicked at what I specialize in. Now get your ass in this elevator." She hated scaring him, but he needed to understand she was in charge; that, and she couldn't keep allowing him to tempt her. Shyness was one thing—

she found it cute. But fear? Fear brought out the monster in her.

They travelled down in silence, and when Anthony entered his lab, she followed him. When he darted a look at her, she again bared the smile that freaked him out. "Don't mind me. I've decided, given your inability to follow common sense where you safety is concerned, I'd better stick close by."

He grunted in reply and then proceeded to ignore her as he flicked on monitors and read the screen results.

"Impossible," he mumbled.

Curious, Lexie wandered over to see what had his briefs in a knot. "What's up?"

"The results of your DNA test."

Lexie froze. She'd heard mention of her DNA the day before, but ignored it because she'd figured she misunderstood. "Where did you get my DNA?"

Anthony flashed her a brief look she didn't understand before concentrating on the screen again. "I came home covered in it when you got shot."

"And, what? You just decided to use it?" Panic fluttered in her breast. The decision to tell him or not about her alter ego was no longer a choice. Her secret was about to see the light of day because of bloody science.

He shrugged. "I thought you were dead. It was my way of preserving a part of you. Anyway, the how and why I got it aren't the interesting parts. What I'd like to figure out is why your DNA is twined with that of a wolf's?"

"A wolf's?" Lexie's laughter sounded brittle even to her. "That's crazy."

"Exactly, and yet...there's no denying it. Somehow my samples got contaminated with wolf genes and, even stranger, they merged with yours in a most fascinating double helix."

"Wow, that is weird." Lexie walked away lest her relief at his obliviousness become too obvious.

"It's weird alright, but at the same time, it gave me a fantastic idea on how to deal with Mr. Thibodeaux's condition."

And with those words, her geek went to work, bustling from work station to machine, to computer then back. Lexie perched on a stool and kept one eye on him as she used her BlackBerry to check on emails and other items that required her attention. She also tapped back into the lab's security network, checking for anomalies and weaknesses in the system. During her middle of the night check, she'd easily hacked into the main system using some blackmarket hacker apps and added herself, along with a few surprises.

A few hours after their arrival in the lab, a buzzer sounded and Lexie jumped up, glad to have a reason to move.

Anthony peered over at her and smirked. "That's just the lunch bell."

"Oh." She scowled at him. "Well, come on then. I'm hungry."

"And if I say I'd rather stay and work?"

Lexie's stomach rumbled and shredded her patience.

"Unless you want me to embarrass you by carrying you over my shoulder to eat, then you'd better pause whatever you're doing."

"Oh, please. Like you could carry me."

"You'd be surprised at what I can do," she muttered under her breath. Thankfully, she didn't have to show him because he typed a few keystrokes then came toward her. She ignored how cute he looked with his hair standing up wildly in Einstein fashion, and how his blue eyes shone with excitement. She clamped her desire down tight and followed him as he led the way to a secure room setup as a dining area, replete with a dining table and another large window overlooking the grounds.

Lexie sat him at one end of the table and then positioned herself square in the middle facing the view outdoors. She wanted a direct line of sight just in case.

Dishes covered in silver domes waited amidst cutlery and napkins. Lexie slapped Anthony's hand away and lifted the covers, sniffing the food for traces of poison.

Anthony assumed she smelled for a different reason. "Smells like chef outdid himself, and look, no mini assassins are waiting on my plate."

Lexie shot him a dark look even as her lip curled at his sarcastic humor. She'd enjoyed shy Anthony at the conference, then the confident one, but this new sarcastic side intrigued her. It proved he had a backbone hidden somewhere inside his geeky body.

Seated in front of olfactory heaven, Lexie dove in. The chef thankfully knew how to prepare his beef and Lexie groaned as she chewed, her tongue and taste buds dancing as they met red meat heaven. Anthony stared at her as she devoured her meal and after a few bites she stopped. "What?"

Shaking his head as if startled, he dropped his gaze. "Sorry, just wondering about a few things."

"Such as?" She asked feigning disinterest as she resumed her meal.

"Do you live around here when you're not working?"

"Kind of. I've got a place in the city, but it's more a crash pad than anything else."

"What about family?"

She stopped eating again and gave him a pointed look. "What's with all the questions?"

He shrugged. "Just making polite conversation and wondering how your parents feel about renting yourself out."

The jibe stung and, as if ashamed of his comment, Anthony ducked his head, but he couldn't hide the red creeping up his neck. She bit back a smile. *My geek has more backbone than I keep giving him credit for.* "My mom keeps waiting for me to settle down, but I'm not the type." Her mom also lamented the fact her daughter had a brain and wouldn't do her duty to the pack. As for her dad, he just muttered that she'd settle down once the right wolf came along who could beat the stubbornness out of her. And they wondered why she avoided coming over to visit.

The conversation stalled, and Lexie concentrated on filling her belly. She scraped the last bite off her plate and leaned back with a happy sigh. "That chef is a bloody genius."

Her happy belly held her as Anthony spent the next few hours in the lab. Boredom set in quickly as she watched Anthony bury himself in his work. To keep herself entertained, she did yoga, stretching her limbs and arching her body in complicated poses which relaxed her.

"Must you do that," he sputtered after a while.

Lexie, pretzeled into a yoganidrasana position, grunted. "I'm bored and I need exercise."

"Fine, then we'll hit the gym. I need a break anyhow."

Unfolding herself carefully, Lexie's keen sight didn't miss the tent in Anthony's pants. *I guess it wasn't what I was doing that bugged him, but the fact he wanted to do me.* Her nipples tightened at the thought.

He brought her to a new part of the building which housed a state of the art gym. Her geek stripped his coat and dress shirt off, leaving him clad only in his slacks and a t-shirt. He set the treadmill and began to run, his eyes closed in concentration. Just as eager to ignore him, Lexie hit the weights, exerting her muscles as a way of ignoring her other bodily needs.

After a while, a prickling sense let her know he watched her.

"What?" she asked through gritted teeth, hefting the weight.

"Um, you're awfully strong."

Determined to give herself a good workout, Lexie hadn't paid attention to the fact she bench pressed more than the average body builder could. Honestly, she hadn't really expected Anthony to notice or know the difference.

"It's all about technique," she lied, getting up off the bench and heading towards the punching bag.

"Why is it I get the impression there's more to you than meets the eye?" he murmured aloud.

Lexie didn't answer. Anything she said other than the truth would have probably sounded false.

THEY FELL into a routine over the next few days, one wrought with tension—the sexual kind. She knew he masturbated nightly in the shower, and wished she dared do the same, but she didn't want to risk rousing her passion any more than it already was. The imminent full moon pressed on her and she knew she wasn't completely successful at hiding her hungry gaze around Anthony. And stupid human that he was, he didn't run away.

She successfully fought off her urge to tear his clothes off and fuck him, but the tension in her body took its toll. Even worse, she could tell he fought the same battle.

She had no idea what he did hour after hour in the lab, but she knew he'd made some kind of progress because he worked at a frenzied pace, muttering to himself and working late into the night. Of Frederick, their employer, she saw neither hide nor hair, although she did catch glimpses of his guards and minions. They wisely made a wide berth around her, knowing her reputation—smart because, in her current frame of mind, any wrong move, look or word would have been deadly.

The day of the full moon, Lexie paced restlessly and Anthony looked up from his work long enough to notice. "Are you alright? You're acting like a lion in a cage."

Lexie almost snorted. Change the lion to wolf and he'd hit the problem dead on. "Listen. There's going to be a bit of a change tonight. I've got to go out for a while."

"Going on a date?" Anthony tossed the words at her casually, but she could see the tension in the tight way he gripped his pen.

Jealousy—how yummy. Lexie mentally shook herself. "No, I've got some business to take care of. I want you to lock this place down tight when I leave."

"But how will you get back in?"

"Don't worry about me."

"You know, it's been three days since you arrived and more than that since the attempted kidnapping and shooting at the conference. Don't you think you and the boss are being a tad paranoid?"

She stalked toward him, her wolf side growling when he backed up from her. She crowded him and leaned in close, close enough to smell his fear—and excitement.

"Listen here, my giant geek."

"I really wish you wouldn't call me that."

Lexie lost her patience. She grabbed him by the lapels and pulled him close. "You. Are. In. Danger. Just because you're not seeing the violence directed at you doesn't mean it's not happening. In the days since I've been here, we've intercepted one bomb, two assassins and one really ugly shirt. So do not tell me you're not in danger."

"Uh, if you say so."

This close to him, her emotions swirling, she couldn't stop herself from leaning in the last inch that separated them and pressing her mouth to his. He hesitated at first as she slid her lips along his, her tongue coaxing him to open wide. Lexie, no longer quite in control, pressed herself closer, and gave a grunt of satisfaction at the feel of his hard cock pressing against her belly. It only took a few seconds more before he relaxed, giving her access to his tongue as his arms came to wrap around her.

A fever caught hold of her and she felt her claws and canines extending as her wolf pushed, make that demanded, she claim this man. She wanted to shred his clothes from him and ride him hard, as she sank her teeth into his skin and...

With a snarl, Lexie pushed away from him. She turned and gave him her back, knowing she couldn't hide the changes in her body from him. She didn't dare look at him lest she completely lose her mind and do what her pulsating body demanded. *Fuck him. Mark him. Keep him.* Her wolf's needs and desires came through crystal clear. Lexie fought her inner bitch, but she could feel the tide of the battle shifting away from her, putting Anthony in danger.

"Get up to your apartment, now." She held herself stiffly as she faced away from him.

"I wasn't done with my work here."

She whirled with a growl. "Don't make me knock you out like I did our last night at the conference."

He sucked in a breath and regarded her incredulously. "I didn't pass out like I thought, did I?"

"Pressure points, baby. Now get your sweet cheeks moving before I show you some less pleasant ones." Lexie didn't curb her tone. She needed him to move now. Even though night had only just started to fall, her wolf side pushed at her. Called her to shed her humanity and revel in her animalistic heritage.

She watched him flee and couldn't help pursuing him, his prey-like action clashing with her desire to possess him. She stalked him down the hall as he scurried to enter the elevator. He paused at the threshold. He turned around and tossed her a strange look—*was that defiance I saw on his face?* The doors slid shut before she could chase him down and reiterate the need for him to stay away from her and remain safe behind as many locked doors as possible. Assassins and enemies of their boss weren't the only danger to him tonight.

She loped down the hall towards the emergency stairs. She slapped her hand on the console and for a second feared her elongated nails would fuck up the reading, but the electronic portal whisked open and she barreled down the stairs, her need to run wild pulsing just below her skin.

Two more hand scans and she made it outside. Quickly, she whirled and keyed in the lockdown code—the new one that her geek didn't have access to. She didn't trust him to not try and disable it to return to his lab.

Silvery fingers of moonlight tickled across her

exposed skin and Lexie turned to drink them in. She let her jacket slide from her shoulders to drop to the ground. She kicked off her boots and shimmied out of her pants. Her top and panties quickly followed suit. Naked, she strode forward, ignoring the niggling warning that she should move to the back of the building where there were fewer eyes.

But her wolf drove now, and it had no shame. It rejoiced in the call of the moon. Paced with a frenzy as the time to run—to be free—fast approached.

Bathed in moonlight, Lexie let out a long sigh as she gave up the fight to hold her inner self back. Her skin rippled, a painful thing that made her cry out, and then scream as her limbs cracked and shifted, reshaping her. Her screaming cry of pain transitioned in pitch until she stood there on four feet and howled.

Time to hunt.

CHAPTER TWENTY

ANTHONY RODE the elevator up to his apartment trembling. Part of it was fear if he were to be honest with himself, but the rest had to do with what he'd just seen. Something possessed Lexie, or had always been a part of her if he could believe the tests he'd run.

With her living in such close proximity to him, it proved ridiculously easy for him to snag DNA samples in the form of saliva from her toothbrush and hair from her pillow with follicles still attached. Each test, no matter which way or how many times he ran it, came back the same. Lexie's genetic code was not one hundred percent human. His discovery of the double helix of human DNA twined with wolf belonged to her. He'd assumed the anomaly was a dormant portion of her genetic makeup, until a few moments ago in his lab where she'd *changed*.

Even as clueless as he usually found himself around

women and their moods, he'd noticed a strange energy imbuing Lexie all day, an almost sizzling current that emanated from her, strong enough it made the hair on his body stand on end. He'd watched her with wary eyes, unable to help himself, intrigued—and in lust—with the wild animal magnetism that rolled off her while she moved about his space with predatory grace. Anthony feared her coiled tension and leashed violence, almost physically visible beneath the veneer of her indomitable will, but his trepidation wasn't the only thing flooding his senses. Her dominant persona drew him, made him want to beg her to share that passionate energy, to touch him and let him taste it. When she finally did, with a kiss so scorching he'd expected to implode, he'd almost come in his pants. Then just about crapped them when he'd felt her change.

When she'd kissed him, he'd felt, to his shocked disbelief, how her canines had elongated, and the way her nails seemed to suddenly sharpen into razor points. Even more astonishing, he'd seen the way her eyes glowed. She hadn't needed to threaten him to get him to flee, he was ready to do that on his own as myths he'd scoffed at tumbled around in his mind, making a mockery of his assertions that creatures of the night didn't exist.

He attempted to cling to disbelief, to wrap tight around him the rules governing science. Perhaps in his fear of her strange mood, he'd imagined or exaggerated some of the things he'd perceived. People couldn't grow fangs and their eyes definitely didn't shine with an inner light, and the woman he'd once made love to most assuredly wasn't a werewolf, even if her DNA seemed to want to say otherwise.

Then why did I run away?

Anthony moved across his darkening living room and leaned his head on the glass overlooking the front of the building, the soft glow of the moon bathing him in a pale radiance. His eyes fluttered shut as he sought to control his rampaging imagination, but a motion outside caught him before his lids fully closed.

Peering down, he saw Lexie. He forgot to breathe as he watched her strip until she stood naked, her body a thing of beauty. Head held high, she walked forward, away from the building, the light from the moon along with the security lights behind her illuminating her bare shape. And then despite all his scientific knowledge, despite everything he believed in, he saw the impossible.

Her whole body rippled as if alive. His stomach churned at the sickening movement on her flesh that brought to mind alien movies he'd watched in his youth because, just like those horror movies, it appeared as if something tunneled under her skin and fought to escape. Under his riveted gazed, her skin darkened as fur sprouted spontaneously while, at the same time, her limbs contorted. As if that weren't horrifying enough, through the tempered glass he could hear her strident screams, her rapid change from woman to beast an obviously painful ordeal.

When the agonized cry transformed into a howl, the truth hit Anthony like a freight train, refuting every logical assumption he'd ever made. Lexie was a werewolf just like her DNA touted.

He slumped to the floor in disbelief as the woman he'd made love to bound off into the darkness of the trees his boss kept on the premises. An eternity passed as he stared out into the night, his mind a clean slate as his psyche adjusted to his sudden, new reality. Shock could only last so long before his brain and common sense kicked in. *So what if I've discovered that the impossible is real. This is a moment to celebrate, to explore a new frontier.* How many scientists could boast they'd been given the chance to research a live werewolf? And yet, here he sat like a dolt, staring at nothing.

Eagerness to not let this opportunity escape made him spring from the floor and head to his bedroom to change. He dressed in dark clothes and found a navy colored hat. Snatching his digital camera, which he set for night-time photography, he moved to the elevator and slapped his hand on the console. The light flashed red and a message scrolled onto the screen.

System Lockdown.

Lexie had locked him in. Or so she thought. Anthony didn't spend much time attempting to get around her lockdown code. Why, when he already had an alternate escape route for the times he needed to spend time alone without guards or cameras watching him.

The fire exit to his apartment hid behind a large pantry in his kitchen. He'd hidden it early on in his tenure and programmed it to run on its own network. He slid the heavy furniture to the side, revealing the door and security panel. When he tapped his hand to the scanner, the light turned green and Anthony grinned.

He jogged down the dark stairs, excitement bubbling in him. He reached the bottom and with another slap of his hand, opened the door to the outside. Hidden behind dense brush, Anthony fought his way through until he stood in the clear. It was only as he viewed the dark tree line that he wondered how he'd find Lexie. Mr. Thibodeaux's property spanned over a hundred acres, a good portion of it wooded. He refused to allow discouragement to bring him down. Somehow, he'd find her.

Anthony searched the darkness for some of the guards that usually lurked, but not seeing any, he sprinted across the grounds to the shelter of the forest. The white light from the moon didn't reach under the dense canopy of branches and Anthony stumbled for some time through the underbrush like an idiot before halting.

How the hell am I going to find her? At this rate, I'm more likely to twist an ankle than document her. The easy and probably smart solution involved him returning to his apartment and confronting Lexie in the morning. However, Anthony grew tired of always taking the safe route. All his life, he'd followed rules whether of science or society's making. Tonight, for the first time in his life, he realized that rules didn't need to apply, not if he wanted to live life to the fullest and truly discover things. In order to open his mind, he needed to leave his comfort zone and confront the unknown, starting with one intriguing werewolf in the woods.

His enthusiastic inner pep talk held him for a while as he tread through the forest; however, the further he went, the more the icy grip of fear tried to clutch him. His neck prickled as if eyes watched him. His skin grew cold and clammy as the gloom hugged him tight and mocked him for his inability to see further than a few feet in front of him.

He stood still, his heart racing, and listened to the sounds of the night, but he had to admit, he had no idea what the heck he expected to hear. The outdoors wasn't exactly his strong point and he grew tired of tracking her, if his feeble attempt could be termed such. It occurred to him that while he couldn't discern her presence, with her probably heightened senses, she could more aptly find him, especially if she were made aware her charge had escaped the building she'd imprisoned him in.

Taking in a deep breath and ignoring his manly pride, which at this point was mostly swallowed by fatigue and fear, he bellowed for her. "Lexie!"

A hush seemed to descend over the forest, and he shivered as he reminded himself there was nothing to fear. The woods on Mr. Thibodeaux's lands were not truly in the wilds with any number of feral creatures; although, Lexie's assertion that his life was in peril came back to haunt him. In leaving the lab to satisfy curiosity had he painted a target on himself? And now, by bellowing like some idiot, pinpointing his location, was he signing his own death warrant?

Fear descended on him, a blanketing cold that amplified every noise, from the crackle of underbrush to the slight whistle of the wind through the branches. His heart rate sped up as the darkness became cloying, and he whirled, sensing more than one predatory gaze on him, yet he saw nothing. He started to walk, his steps noisy compared to the quiet that had fallen because even the whirring of the insects ceased. Soon, his slow steps turned into a paced jog, then a full out run. Something roamed out there in the shadows. Irrational as it seemed, Anthony could sense it there, a dark hunter watching him hungrily.

Anthony crashed through the shrub, almost losing his balance several times in his headlong flight. Around him, the sounds of chase erupted as those stalking him dropped their pretense of hiding. His breathing hitched and sweat poured all over his body as he pumped his legs faster, cursing his own stupidity in not listening to Lexie. She'd warned him about leaving the building. Warned him that things waited for their moment to harm him, but like the stupid blonde in the movies, the one he used to mock, he'd not obeyed. And now, like the victim of a horror flick, he ran for his life.

He saw the welcoming glow of building lights, closer than expected, and he didn't take the time to hear his mind mocking him over walking in circles; in this instance he thanked his ineptness as it meant safety loomed nearer than expected. He strained harder to reach the haven he should have never left. He hit the edge of the woods and stumbled out into the cleared area. The nightmare followed him with snarls.

Anthony reached the main door to his lab and

slapped his hand on the console only to have the lock-down warning flash.

"No," he whispered. He'd forgotten about Lexie's extra security. He whirled around to move to his secret exit, but froze as he encountered a line of beasts moving toward him.

Anthony backed against the door, riveted in fear as three large wolves stalked towards him, their eyes glowing balefully. He could hear their low growls and see their raised hackles as they approached. He scanned them, desperately looking for Lexie, whose pelt, he recalled, gleamed a solid black; however, she didn't appear to number among the approaching wolves.

Standing and waiting to get eaten wouldn't save him. His only chance at survival involved him making it to that damned exit. He shuffled his feet and almost tripped over Lexie's clothing. His foot nudged a hard lump and he chanced a quick look down. He almost gibbered in relief when he saw the revolver. Quickly, he stooped to grab it and pointed it with shaking hands at the encroaching beasts.

"Stop," he whispered. Then louder, "Stop it, or I'll shoot." Why he assumed the creatures would listen he didn't analyze. Perhaps it was the cunning intelligence in their eyes that made him realize these wolves hadn't sprung forth as a cubs, or their immense size which made it seem more likely he'd found more werewolves. If they understood, then they chose to ignore his command. Squeezing his eyes shut, Anthony pulled the trigger. The loud crack of the gunshot rang loud, and

Anthony pried an eye open to see if he'd scared the beasts.

Nope. They still approached, but now he could swear he saw disdain in their eyes. Given he couldn't shoot worth a damn, Anthony went to plan B—*run*.

Before he could weigh the pros and cons of that action, he moved, sprinting across the front of the building. He might as well have waved a red cape. Vicious snarls erupted as the beasts charged him. Anthony pumped his legs harder, even as he knew he'd already lost the race.

A heavy weight hit him in the back, and he fell, his knees meeting the ground painfully. Teeth snapped as Anthony rolled, trying to move away from the creature determined to kill him. Sharp, burning pain raked his left arm as something latched on. Anthony gasped at the fiery agony. He tried to pull away, but a heavy weight sat on him as the jaw holding his arm shook it back and forth, toying with him.

A piercing howl caught his attention, but not for long considering the more pressing problem of the wolf trying to chew his arm off. Another howl erupted, its chilling challenge even closer. The creature using his arm as a chew toy bounded off his back and Anthony waited for the attack to resume on a new body part; however, while he heard snarling, it seemed to have moved away from him. He turned his head, the waves of pain radiating from his arm threatening to pull him down into darkness. He blinked at what he saw. The three wolves who'd cornered him were fighting a fourth with sleek black fur.

Lexie. She'd arrived to save him, and now, fought for her life. Anthony struggled to his knees, his wounded arm hanging limp and useless at his side, his glasses cracked and sitting skewed on his face. He watched as she snapped at the other wolves, her sharp fangs drawing blood and yelps. Her fluid movements mesmerized him, for not only did she show no fear, she was savagely beautiful. And even more astonishing, gaining the upper hand.

The wolves attacking her got wise to her tactics and circled her. Anthony wanted to yell when they charged her all at once, but he feared distracting her. Horrified fascination froze his gaze on the battle, and anguish pierced him as her fur became matted with blood. *Useless, I'm freaking useless.* Even if his arm weren't a throbbing piece of ruined flesh, he'd have had nothing to offer help-wise. He didn't have super strength or teeth or anything to help her, but he also couldn't kneel there like a coward watching her fight alone. *Hold on, I do have something to even the odds. The gun.* He'd dropped it in his tussle with the wolves, but he quickly spotted it on the ground. He grasped it and staggered to his feet, gritting his teeth at the cascading pain.

Once on his feet though, he ran into a dilemma. He couldn't shoot well enough to aid her; although, even the poorest shooter could score if close enough to its target. Refusing to analyze the stupidity of his action, Anthony staggered over to the snapping furry melee and aimed a kick at one of the attacking wolves. As kicks went, it sucked, but it served its purpose in getting that particular wolf's attention. It turned to face him with a snarl and Anthony aimed the gun. He fired, the loud crack not stifling the yelp as he hit the damned wolf. He didn't get a chance to see the damage though, as the recoil from the fired shot sent him reeling.

Anthony hit the ground, and ended up splayed flat on his back, staring at the spinning sky. As he lost the battle with the darkness creeping over his vision, he prayed Lexie survived his stupidity.

CHAPTER TWENTY-ONE

LEXIE PACED FREDERICK'S OFFICE, the metal shutters pulled tight against the encroaching dawn light. Her employer hung up his phone and glared at her. "You almost allowed my asset to die."

"Me? It was your fucking minions who tried to take a piece out of him. If you can't control your dogs, then maybe I should put them down permanently." She allowed her anger to fill her. It beat the alternative of anguish when she'd seen Anthony fighting for his life.

"I thought you were supposed to have him locked up tighter than the president's daughter?"

"Apparently, our resident geek had a secret exit, one he wiped from the building schematics housed on the computer." *Brilliant fucking idiot.*

"I don't pay you for excuses," Frederick snarled.

"Fine. Then don't pay me at all." Lexie couldn't

believe she'd said that, but once spoken, she didn't take the words back.

"What? You're quitting?"

Lexie braced her hands on his desk and leaned forward, her lips curled in a sneer. "You wish, dead dick. I'm still going to guard, Anthony, because the idiot needs me, not because you're paying me." Besides, she'd made enough in the last few days to cover her for a few months, that and she felt guilty for failing Anthony. While she'd technically done her job to the best of her abilities, she'd fucked up. She should have known about the secret exit and, even with the moon change, never left off guarding the perimeter of the building. If she'd stayed closer instead of haring off on a run to clear her mind, Anthony's attack could have been averted.

"Well, in that case then, do whatever you wish. I'm not going to argue a free bodyguard." Frederick leaned back in his chair and crossed his arms, the smirk on his face begging for a slap.

"You're still feeding me though," she grumbled as she stalked out of his office and back to the building housing the lab and apartment.

She walked with quick steps, her mind whirring with the developments of the last twelve hours. First and foremost, she'd discovered she loved the damned geek. Sure, she'd realized she cared for him, even liked him, but when she'd seen him, struggling to stay alive as he hovered so close to death, it hit her hard—*I love the stupid, human nerd.*

Not that it changed anything. She was still a were-

THE GEEK JOB   137

wolf and he a fragile human. Even if she pretended she could control herself, she knew it was only a matter of time before she forgot herself and killed him in the throes of passion. Her nature just wouldn't allow her to play nice forever.

And even if she thought she could make her bitch behave, she also assumed Anthony wouldn't want to come near her after discovering her furry side. For all she knew, he'd left the safety of the building to escape because she'd stupidly allowed her wolf to take charge in full sight of the building. Perhaps a subconscious act on her part to relate the truth?

At least now, if he still wanted her after discovering her hairy problem, he'd understand what she meant when she told him they couldn't be together. Now, if only the thought of his rejection didn't fill her with sorrow.

She arrived at his apartment and relieved the guard inside. The human doctor whom Frederick kept on staff to tend his sheep, straightened from Anthony's bedside.

"How's he doing?" she asked, her eyes anxiously scanning her geek's pale face. She winced at the thick bandages wrapping his left side.

"He'll live, but whether he keeps the arm or not is anyone's guess. I've done the best I can, stitching the flesh up and cleaning it. I've also dosed him with painkillers and antibiotics."

She gnawed her lip, not encouraged by the doctor's blunt assessment. "When will he wake?"

The doctor shrugged. "When his body feels ready.

I've left some drugs for the pain on his nightstand. I'll be back in about eight hours to change his dressing."

Lexie nodded and saw the man out before she returned to keep vigil. As she stared down at Anthony, lying so still, she wished there were a way to impart her shifter healing powers on him. However, unlike legends, werewolf status was something her kind were born with, not a mutation caused by bites. *How I wish it were different. If I could make him a werewolf, not only would his arm heal, we could also be together.* Wishful thinking though wouldn't change reality.

Lexie paced at the foot of the bed, waiting for Anthony to regain consciousness so she could tear him a new one. She thought back on the harrowing moments of the night before. It still amazed her that Anthony had found enough courage even after his injury to take on one of the wolves himself. Lexie would have prevailed in the long run, but when the number of assailants suddenly dropped to two, she dispatched them quickly. But that ended up only the start of a long night. She'd stood over her geek's prone body, guarding his nerdy ass from Frederick's resident shifters who had poor control of their beast side and also from the younger vamps who'd smelt the blood and come running.

Finally, someone not out to try and fight her or eat him showed up and she led them to Anthony's secret entrance. Frederick himself had arrived as Anthony was placed on his bed and tended the wounds himself, totally grossing Lexie out. Frederick had licked the bloody gashes, the coagulant in his saliva stopping the bleeding and at the same time releasing agents to speed the healing process, an inborn vampire defense mechanism that fooled victims in doubting they'd been attacked. However, all the vampire spit in the world couldn't heal the deep, bloody gouges covering Anthony's arm. The doctor arrived and went to work with his needle, but Lexie knew enough about wounds to guess that Anthony's arm would require a miracle to remain attached.

It wasn't until early evening that he finally stirred with a groan. Acting on intuition, she knelt at his side and supported his head up, offering him a straw to sip water. He swallowed, his eyes shut as his throat worked, pulling the liquid. He spat the straw out when done and she lowered his head back down to his pillow. She stood and watched as he fluttered eyes with thicker lashes than she'd noticed before.

It took him a moment to focus and she waited to see what he'd say. Hopefully, nothing along the lines of, "Argh, werewolf!" That would probably crush her.

"Lexie," he whispered.

"Yes, Anthony."

"You're safe. Thank the gods of science." He closed his eyes with a smile.

Lexie snapped. "Don't you dare go back to sleep, Anthony. I want to know what the fuck you were thinking, leaving the apartment yesterday after I expressly told you not to."

He opened one eye to peer at her. "I wanted to take pictures of you."

"Of all the stupid things," she muttered. "And it couldn't wait until I came back?"

He shrugged, then winced. "Ow. I guess the part about my arm getting chewed on is real, too. Why didn't you tell me you were a werewolf?"

She wanted to slap him for having a one track, curious mind. "Shouldn't your first question be how bad is your arm?"

Anthony gave her a wan smile. "I know it's bad. My guess would be if infection sets in, I'll lose it."

"And that doesn't bother you?" Lexie wanted to check him for a fever. She expected hysterics, sobbing, denial even, but this calm acceptance freaked her out.

"I'm more worried about you. You took a beating from those wolves. Are you okay?"

Lexie gaped at him. He'd lost his fucking mind in the attack. That had to be it. "I'm fine. See." She lifted her shirt and whirled, flashing her already closed wounds, the red weals the only remaining sign of the attack.

"Wow. That's impressive. I don't suppose I'll turn into a werewolf now that I've gotten chomped on?"

He sounded so hopeful. She sighed. "Sorry. Legend only. Werewolves are born, not made."

"I see." He seemed to ponder this for a moment, and she thought he'd gone back to sleep when he said, "So, is it the fact I'm human that keeps you from being with me?"

"What makes you think I even want you?"

A flush crept up his cheeks. "My mistake. I assumed the tension between us was sexual in nature."

Lexie thought about lying, but she just couldn't do that to him anymore. "You weren't mistaken. I don't know why, but I want you." Before he could speak, she held up her hand. "But it can't happen. Our time at the conference was wonderful, I won't deny that. However, that gentle side of me isn't the norm. Having sex with humans requires me being careful, and I can have fun, but while it scratches the itch, it doesn't cure the problem. It can actually compound the urge."

"So things get a little rough."

She glared at him. "A little rough? I am stronger, faster and tougher than you can imagine. If I were to forget myself for even one minute in the throes of passion, I could kill you."

"But what a way to go," he replied wistfully.

"You're fucking nuts," she muttered. "Or the drugs are making you spout stupidity."

He struggled to sit up using his good arm. "Why is it stupid to want to be with you? I feel things for you I've never felt before. I want to be with you."

"It was just good sex."

"Fantastic sex and more. You intrigue me with your smarts that you hide under a tough girl veneer. Your courage and audacity awe and inspire me. Your presence makes me happy."

Tears pricked her eyes at his speech and she turned lest he see them and use them against her. Even if drug induced, his words touched her and made her long for something she couldn't have—him.

CHAPTER TWENTY-TWO

LEXIE SHOT him up with drugs and then left the bedroom, but Anthony didn't mind. She'd given him plenty of food for thought. Over the last while, he'd begun to wonder if their attraction to each other existed only in his hopeful mind. Sure, she'd kissed him the day of the attack, and ended up snuggling him nightly even if she scurried away every morning as if afraid he'd catch her. *Like I wouldn't notice the woman of my dreams molding her curves to me.* Discovering her werewolf status should have sent him screaming in the other direction, but instead he felt as if a great weight had been lifted. Their biological differences kept them apart, not him and his geeky nature.

However, knowing she wanted him but was afraid of killing him didn't bring them any closer to a solution. Actually, the way he saw it, there were only two options

—cure Lexie of her werewolf side which he got the impression she'd probably protest, or he needed to change himself.

The bigger question though, was could it be done? The answer awaited him in his lab where twelve lab rats injected with various nano's—a forbidden technology that Mr. Thibodeaux readily encouraged—would tell him if the genetic disorders he'd located in both his employer and Lexie could be replicated, or reversed.

But how to get to his lab? In his current condition, Lexie wasn't likely to let him go waltzing down to check on his test subjects. At the same time, the more time he waited, the more likely he'd lose his arm. Given the grave consequences, he could deal with her anger.

A great plan, if he hadn't fallen asleep, the effects of the drug drawing him down.

When he woke, he sensed someone watching him. Opening his eyes warily, he saw Mr. Thibodeaux sitting by his bed. "Ah, the scientist awakes. How are you feeling?"

Anthony forwent answering for a question that had come to him while he slept. "Are you a vampire?"

His boss chuckled, and Anthony's cheeks flushed, wondering if he'd perhaps assumed wrongly.

"About time you figured it out. I began to wonder if you were as smart as I'd hoped."

"Not so smart, apparently, given I fell for a woman who was paid to like me." Anthony meant it as a snub. He still hadn't quite forgiven his employer for the subterfuge, even if he'd meant well and had only his personal safety in mind.

"Ah, the luscious Lexie. She's quite the woman isn't she? Or should I say bitch?" At Anthony's glare, Mr. Thibodeaux raised a hand. "Down boy. I referred to her animal status, not her actual attitude. I like kick ass women myself. I do apologize for the girlfriend ruse though. But honestly, you can't tell me you didn't enjoy it?"

"Don't ever do that again. It's demeaning. How would you like it if you found out a woman only had sex with you because she was paid?"

"Fine. I'll concede that point to you. You must be ecstatic now then, that she's refused payment to remain your guard." Frederick finished speaking and watched him, waiting for a reaction.

"What?" Anthony's brow creased as he tried to make sense of his boss's words.

"Lexie told me after your accident there last night that she no longer wished to be paid to be your guard."

"She's leaving?" Panic clawed him. She couldn't leave, not until he'd had a chance to see if he could solve the problem keeping them apart.

Mr. Thibodeaux sighed. "You know, for a smart man you are awfully dense. She's not getting paid, but she's staying. Or in simple terms, since you don't get it—she's staying with you because she likes you, not because of the obscene salary I was paying her."

Anthony's head spun. Despite her objections and

assertion they couldn't be together, she didn't want to leave him. Anthony felt like jumping out of the bed and dancing. He couldn't stop his silly grin when she walked in and with a scowl, she growled, "What's so funny?"

He and his boss laughed as she grumbled about men and their little heads doing their thinking. Mr. Thibodeaux left after assuring him he'd get the best medical care possible for his arm, and a hint about the progress of his sun allergy research. Anthony ignored the blatant probing even though he knew the solution possibly already waited in his lab.

Lexie slammed a tray down with dishes. "Dinner," she announced unnecessarily.

"I need to go to my lab."

She crossed her arms over her chest and smirked. "Not likely. Now eat."

"Just for an hour. I need to check on some mice I injected and run a few tests, else my progress will be moot."

"Eat and we'll see."

Sighing, Anthony picked up a spoon and ate the stew the chef had prepared. Truthfully, the food energized him enough that as soon as she whipped the tray away, he swung his legs out of the bed and stood. He'd forgotten about the drugs though. He swayed as the pain medications made him woozy. Arms wrapped around him, steadying him, and he breathed deep of her scent, his cock twitching at her proximity.

"Idiot," she grumbled.

Given her closeness though, he'd actually have said more like genius. "I ate, now please can we go to my lab. Just for an hour. I promise to do the tests and observations sitting."

"I want it known that I disagree totally with this, and when you faint and I carry you back like some pansy, I'm going to laugh at you."

Anthony didn't take offense. He finally understood her mean verbal attacks were a way of hiding her feelings. And besides, he'd gotten what he wanted.

She slid her arm around his waist and draped his good arm over her shoulder. Anthony didn't really like having to lean on her for help—he did have some pride left after all—but if his fervent wishing came true, soon, she'd be able to lean on him.

The trip down the elevator and up the hall to his lab made his stomach roil and a cold sweat broke out all over his body. A glance over at Lexie showed him tight lips and a furious look in her eyes, but she got him into his lab and seated before she spoke.

"This better be important or I will beat you worse than those wolves did," she growled. "Now, where are those mice?"

Anthony pointed at a door and she wheeled his chair over. They entered and she wrinkled her nose. "Eew. Stinks in here." She peered at the cages and made a moue of disgust. "Mice. Nasty things. I don't know how you can work with them."

"Since they gross you out, why don't you wait outside

then? I just need to take some notes. I'll call you when I'm done."

She threw another glance at his test subjects and shuddered. "Fine. But if they get out, don't expect me to catch them. I'm a wolf, not a fucking cat."

She left and Anthony focused his attention on the animals in the cages. The results astonished him.

He grabbed his clipboard off the metal counter and verified the serial numbers he'd assigned for the different serums. Cage 00011—the two mice injected with an untwisted version of his boss's DNA were unrecognizable, their bodies misshapen, but the horrifying part was their elongated teeth which they'd apparently used to feed off each other in a frenzy before dying. *Okay, reversing the vampiric condition is not a feasible option at this time.*

He went on to the next cage, 00014. Inside, the two mice peered at him with red eyes. He leaned forward and the critters suddenly hissed, displaying pointy fangs as they flung themselves at the bars. *Interesting. I'll have to test and compare their DNA mutations to Mr. Thibodeaux's. If I can provoke the vampiric condition then there must be a way to suppress or eliminate it.*

He'd left the most important cage for last. Inside, only one mouse appeared, grooming itself. Anthony could see pale scars as if the creature had hurt itself, and yet, he knew the previous day the mouse had been unmarked. Excitement began to build in him as he perused the cage for the other specimen. He opened the cage and kept a watchful eye on the live mouse, but it just regarded him placidly. Anthony grabbed the plastic house and upended it. He recoiled at what tumbled out, mostly because of the blood and the deadly wound gaping in the creature's neck. However, fascination had him look past the gore to see the miracle he'd created—a miniature wolf with white fur. Apparently its death had frozen its state. How interesting that even though the moonlight hadn't touched it, the mouse, injected with Lexie's wolf DNA, still changed.

Even more fabulous, it worked. Logic dictated he run some tests, that he duplicate his trial run, that he exercise caution; however, the fiery pain in his arm and the shooting red streaks he could see creeping across his hand let him know time was running out.

Done in here, he debated how to get to the fridge where he'd stored the surplus nano imbued serums. Lexie wouldn't just let him shoot himself up, so he'd just have to get her out of the way for a few minutes.

"I'm done in here," he called.

Keeping her eyes averted from the cages, she strode in and pushed the wheeled chair back out into the main lab area. When she continued towards the door back to the hall, taking him away from where he needed to be, he spoke, "Wait. I'm not quite done. I need you to take cage number 00014 and place it in the solarium. I need to verify the next stage of the sun serum for Mr. Thibodeaux."

She didn't pause. "I'll come back and do it after I get you back to bed."

"No." He almost shouted the word and his vehemence made her spin the chair to face her and her narrowed eyes. "That is, I still need to enter a few things on the computer while you do that. It will only take you a minute and it's just down the hall. Plenty of time to run back if I need you."

She didn't look certain and bit her lip. "Fine. But, you better be done by the time I get back or I'll haul you over my shoulder and carry you off cave girl style."

Anthony wanted to snap at her to stop treating him like a weakling, but he could easily imagine her mocking reply. Like, love or not, she currently held the upper hand when it came to strength.

Not for long though if this works.

He pretended to type one handed as she entered the specimen room. She emerged with her nose wrinkled, dangling the cage. Anthony knew he doomed his mice to death given the sunlight that would arrive in the morning, but their demise was a small price to pay. The door no sooner clicked behind her than he pushed away from his workstation with his one good arm, sending his chair skidding over to the glass door of the fridge. He pulled it open and fumbled through the vials, but the one he wanted was at the back of the tray. He lifted the tray onto his lap and located his prize. He snapped the ampule onto the syringe he'd stashed in his pocket. He didn't think, he didn't contemplate the insanity of his actions, he just jabbed his leg with the needle and depressed the plunger. Unsure if the small dosage he'd given the mice would be enough, he grabbed a second and third vial, injecting each in quick succession.

It was only as he slid the tray back into the fridge that he noticed the third vial wasn't the one for Lexie's Lycan gene, but his boss's vampiric one. Then it was too late to think, as his body went into convulsions and the blood coursing in his veins caught on fire.

CHAPTER TWENTY-THREE

LEXIE DROPPED the cage in the solarium and made a face at the ugly mice inside. They returned her look with baleful red eyed ones of their own. Then they hissed, showing elongated, pointy fangs, and she sucked in a breath.

"Holy fuck, Anthony. What did you do?" Because she somehow knew Frederick hadn't wasted his time turning a pair of mice into little bloodsuckers. She peered at the glassed panels of the solarium and then back at the little critters. Realization bloomed—*he tricked me.*

She took off running back up the hall, a faint crash making her curse and pick up her speed. She slapped her hand on the console and waited for the door to open, each second an eternity. She slipped inside and scanned the room, not immediately seeing him, but she could hear movement. She peered behind the first counter of equipment and vaulted over the second, stumbling in her shock at what she found.

Anthony trembled on the floor, his body in the grips of a seizure. His eyes were rolled back in his head while spittle foamed at his mouth.

"Fuck. Fuck. Fuck." She cursed nonstop as she whipped a pad of paper off the counter and slid it between his teeth so he wouldn't bite off his tongue. She straddled his body, one of her knees pinning his good arm. For his injured arm, she pinned his hand. But that didn't stop him from banging his head off the floor.

She held him down with her body and spotted the vials on the floor along with the syringe.

"What the fuck did you do?" She whispered the words even as understanding dawned. He'd experimented on himself like the mice. *But what will he become, if he survives?*

After what seemed like an eternity, his body ceased thrashing and he lay still under her. She slipped off him and knelt at his side. She debated fetching the doctor, but at the same time, she didn't want to leave him alone. She tugged his glasses off, and smoothed his hair back.

A tremor ran through his body, then another. Her nose prickled as his regular scent changed into something unique. He reminded her of wolf, and yet, he also emitted a disturbing element she'd only noticed around Frederick and other vamps. And yet...Anthony lived. *Not for long, because as soon as he wakes up I'm going to kill him for being stupid.*

He moaned, a low, deep sound that rolled into a growl.

Lexie shivered as the noise touched her and roused her wolf. A flare of lust ignited inside her to her mortification given Anthony's prone state. She stood and walked away to gain some distance and perspective. She heard a whisper of sound and whirled only to find herself captured in arms of steel and pushed back up against a wall.

Startled at the speed of the attack, it took her a moment to register who held her. Anthony peered down at her with eyes that glowed a brilliant blue.

"You smell good," he grumbled. Then he dipped his head to kiss her.

She'd always enjoyed her embraces with Anthony, the heat he could engender. But this? This was like a match igniting the driest of timber. His mouth claimed hers with a passion and power that actually made her knees weak. She clung to him as his hard lips slid over hers, sucking and pulling on her flesh. He thrust his tongue into her mouth and the taste of him made her moan.

He apparently enjoyed her reaction because he ground his hips against her lower belly, his solid erection pressing against her. She clutched at his shoulders, knowing somewhere in the back of her mind that she should be pushing him away, questioning his wellbeing; however, caught up in a maelstrom of lust, she could only burn.

His hands slid down her back to cup and squeeze her

buttocks as his mouth moved lower to suck at the tender skin of her neck. She whimpered when he nipped her and wanted him to do it again, but instead he moved his head back to stare at her possessively. She licked her lips and a tremor went through his body.

Before she could ask him what he'd done, or berate him for his foolish experiment, he moved, tearing her skimpy top with his bare hands and baring her flesh. It was her turn to shudder.

"Mine," he growled. She could only gasp as he ducked his head and his mouth latched onto her bared nipple. He took her tight bud into his mouth and swirled his tongue around it and Lexie cried out in pleasure. While his mouth tortured her nub, his hands got busy unbuckling and tugging down her pants. Her snug bottoms caught around her knees and he stopped yanking them to slide a hand between her thighs, stroking her moist flesh.

He stopped his decadent pleasure of her breast to whirl her around until her backside pressed against his fat dick. A hand in the middle of her back pressed her forward, bending her over and she heard the sound of a zipper lowering. Before she could utter a word—or two like "fuck me"—he'd shoved his hard cock into her.

Lexie yelled as his swollen flesh stretched her, seemingly larger than before. His hands caught her around the hips and he plowed her, his body slapping back and forth against her ass as he drove himself into her. She didn't mind his rough play though. It was just what her body craved. She gasped and panted as his quick thrusts quickly brought her to her peak, and then shoved her over it into a quaking orgasm.

With a bellow that sounded more animal than man, he jetted into her. When she felt the rigid tension leave his body, she opened her mouth to ask him what the fuck just happened, but she heard the sharp crack of a slap before she felt the burning pain on her ass cheek.

"Get upstairs, woman. We're not done."

She just about came again at his domineering words and tone. But he was mistaken if he thought she'd give into his orders without a delicious fight.

CHAPTER TWENTY-FOUR

ANTHONY LAUGHED when she threw an indignant glare at him over her shoulder. He slapped her ass again just because he could, and besides, even if she tried to deny it, he could smell the fact she enjoyed it.

The scent of her lust was actually what drew him from the earlier agony of his body's change. His nano injected serums had coursed through his body like wildfire, mutating his body at a molecular level. While he couldn't be sure the extent of his new abilities, he'd definitely noticed an enhancement in his olfactory sense. Like the most evocative of perfumes, her arousal had woken him and driven him to his feet to claim her. He'd opened his lenseless eyes, to discover a sharpened sight beyond anything he'd ever imagined.

As he'd captured her in his arms and with his mouth, he'd vaguely noticed the speed with which he moved, but he'd found himself more intrigued by his dominating need to fuck her, to claim her body.

A distant part of him recognized this new aggressiveness was probably a side effect, but Anthony didn't fight it or care. He'd always wished he could be more assertive, but fear had held him back. Now he feared *nothing*.

Lexie moved away from him, trying to yank up her pants which made her breasts bob enticingly. Anthony stalked toward her and noticed how her breathing hitched.

"Take them off," he ordered.

"Like fuck. What the hell happened to you? I came back to find you doing the worm on hot asphalt dance and now you're acting like you're hopped up on steroids and Viagra."

Anthony let a slow smile creep across his face and he made sure she noticed his new dentition. Her eyes widened and he chuckled. "You said you couldn't be with me unless I was like you. Guess what, darling? I'm now just as much wolf as you are."

She shook her head. "That's impossible. Lycans are born, not made."

"Lycanthropy never counted on a geek who wanted to bang his woman."

His words made her eyes dilate and once again, the waft of her desire tickled his nose. "I want you," he said softly. *And not just in my bed, but in my life forever.* He didn't say those words aloud, knowing she wasn't ready for them—yet.

She shook her head. "You're not just wolf though. If I didn't know better, I'd say you've got some vampire in there, too."

Anthony cocked his head. "A regrettable error. Or not. I'll admit, I panicked when I realized my gaffe, but now..." He used his right hand to tear the bandages off his left revealing smooth skin with only faint red lines to remind him of his maiming. He flexed his healed arm, his muscles bulging, and grinned. "Now, I think that cocktail was just right."

"Shouldn't you be running some tests on your condition?" She moistened her lips with the tip of her pink tongue and Anthony took a step forward, determined to claim those lips for himself.

"The only test I'm running tonight is how many times I can fuck you before we both pass out from exhaustion. I suggest, if you want to do it on a bed that you get your sweet ass moving this instant or you're going to find the floor awfully chilly."

Lexie regarded him for one silent moment before kicking her boots off and shoving her pants down to her ankles. She stepped out of them and kicked them away. She stood there naked, her nipples pebbling, desire rolling off her in a thick wave he could almost grasp. She cocked her hip as she placed a hand on it provocatively. Anthony's cock hardened and he took a step forward.

"Come and get it then if you think you can handle me." She moved fast, darting away from him and leaping over the metal counters. Her hand slapped the console to unlock the door and she exited, sprinting. Anthony grinned as he gave her a five second head start. Then he took off after her.

And when he caught her, she was so fucked.

CHAPTER TWENTY-FIVE

LEXIE RAN up the hall to the elevator, not really trying to escape Anthony, but, given his suddenly dominant attitude, she wasn't just going to roll over and give him her belly—even if she couldn't wait until he took her cunt.

He gave her a head start, but it wasn't enough, not with his new super speed. He caught her before the elevator, swooping her up with one brawny arm that had grown since his change. She shrieked as he threw her over his shoulder then moaned as his hand slid between her thighs to rub against her wet folds.

She noticed he'd shed the remains of his clothing before catching her, and she let her fingers trail over his taut buttocks. She still didn't understand how he'd managed it, but somehow her geeky scientist had not only made the change into wolf—with some vamp mojo for extra speed and strength—but he'd also transitioned into an alpha. Her wolf was beside herself in her mind, yipping and barking about claiming him as their mate.

But Lexie, despite her body and wolf's longings, determined he'd have to pass the same test as the others. If he could best her, then he could have her. She creamed herself at the prospect.

They entered the elevator and Anthony's finger slid into her and she gasped as he found her g-spot and stroked it. He withdrew his hand, to her disappointment, and growled.

"What?" she murmured.

"They're watching." He shifted his weight to balance up on the balls of his feet and a crunching sound filled the cab as Anthony destroyed the camera.

"Frederick won't like that."

"Frederick can kiss my ass if he wants to see sunlight ever again."

Lexie almost giggled. Somehow she didn't think Frederick would be as impressed with this new take charge Anthony. She, on the other hand, found his new persona even more titillating than his previously shy and geeky one.

She didn't make her move until they reached his apartment. She twisted and flipped herself over his shoulder, landing on her feet. She ran and bounded over the couch before she turned to face him with a grin.

"What are you doing?" he barked.

"I have this policy when dealing with male wolves. If you want to have me, first you have to best me."

A slow, wicked smile spread across his face and he

took slow measured steps toward her. "Sounds like fun. How do I know when I've won?"

"If you can bite me at the moment of orgasm, marking me, then I'm yours. But keep in mind, Lycans mate for life. So be very sure before you do this. Once you claim me, there's no turning back."

Her words didn't slow him, but they did make his cock thicken and bob in a distracting manner. "Perfect. Prepare to become mine."

"Cocky geek," she taunted.

"Confident master," he retorted making her knees tremble in a way she'd never expected any man to accomplish.

In the blink of an eye, he went from almost eight feet away to standing in front of her. She just managed to evade his hands, dashing into the bedroom. Again though, his speed overtook her and she found herself swept up into his arms, cradled against his chest. She expected him to fling her onto the bed and have his wicked way with her, but instead he headed for the bathroom. What a letdown.

"What are you doing?"

"Washing my dinner."

Said meal clenched tight. She waited until he put her down in the hot shower before she attempted to escape him again, a failed endeavor, as he caught her before she even set one foot out of the stall. He upended her over his shoulder again, one arm holding her legs firmly as the other spread the lips of her cleft and let the water pour against her sex.

Lexie squealed and pounded at his back and buttocks as he manhandled her with ease. She'd already gone past the point of no return, but she still planned to make a good show of it, loving the way he handled her with ease.

They were both dripping wet and squeaky clean when he carried them back to the bedroom. He dumped her on the bed, but before she could spring up, his body covered hers. Lexie moaned at the hot and heavy feel of his form plastered to hers. His mouth clashed with hers in a fiery kiss that sent electric tingles to her cleft. When she would have twined her arms around his neck, conceding his superior strength, he gathered them in one of his and pushed them above her head. For a moment, she panicked and pulled at her trapped hands, but they didn't budge.

Submission to a male was a new thing for Lexie, and to her surprise, it made her cream.

He grunted against her mouth and moved his lips away to rub his unshaven jaw against her skin. "I can't wait to sink into you."

"Then what are you waiting for?" Lexie gave up fighting. Anthony was who she wanted, and now that the barrier of their species had been torn down, she found herself eager to have him claim her. And to claim him in return.

"You are going to beg me to fuck you," he said before nibbling his way down her neck.

His cocky words made her taunt him. "Then you'd better shut up and get to work."

He nipped her skin in response and Lexie arched as a

jolt of desire shot through her body. He sucked at her flesh, pulling at the skin, leaving a hickey for sure, but he didn't attempt to bite her although he teased her with the edge of his canines. Using his tongue to trace his way, he moved down her body a bit, laving a path between her breasts. He didn't let go of her hands as his mouth brushed over her nipples. He blew on them, his warm breath tightening her nubs. Cream pooled in her cleft as he teased her. Around and around, he kept moving, circling her nipples, never quite touching them. Lexie bit her tongue before she begged him to suck them—or even better, bite them.

He did neither. Yanking her hands down, he pinned them to her stomach as he crawled backwards, his chin brushing against her trimmed pubes. Her cleft quivered, anticipation coiling it tight as she waited for him to eat her like he'd promised. He didn't. He pressed his mouth to the soft skin of her thighs, nipping and kissing, left then right.

Lexie panted with need, but she refused to ask. As if sensing her inner war, he chuckled, his warm breath feathering across her moist lips, unleashing an involuntary moan from Lexie.

"Tell me what you want," he murmured, his lips a bare hairsbreadth away from her core.

Lexie clenched her eyes tight, fighting his allure out of pure stubbornness. She shook her head, unwilling to give in so easily.

He flicked his tongue against her clit, a swift, scorching motion that made her cry out. "Admit you want me to touch you. To lick your sweet pussy until you come on my tongue."

She made the mistake of opening her eyes and gazing down at him. His magnetic blue gaze caught hers and his lips tilted in a seductive grin. She caved to her needs and the pleasure he promised.

"Make me come."

Apparently those three words were enough. He swiped her with his tongue, a long wet lick that made her shiver from head to toe. He spread her lips and jabbed into her core, lapping at her cream. While his one hand held her own down, a prisoner to his delightful torture, his other roamed freely. He used the pad of his thumb to rub her clit while his mouth sucked and tugged on her lips. Lexie's head thrashed and she moaned as he pleasured her. His tongue took the place of his thumb, flicking her clit in a rapid back and forth motion that had her hips bucking. He slid fingers into her sex—one, two, then a tight third. In and out they pumped, as his mouth worked her swollen nub.

After the past few days of abstinence, her climax came fast and hard. Anthony grunted with satisfaction as her pelvic muscles clamped his digits tight.

The tremors hadn't ceased when he moved, his body covering hers. His hands yanked hers back up above her head in a move meant to show he still held control. She loved it.

He settled himself between her thighs and the tip of his dick rubbed against her cleft. "Beg me for it," he growled.

Lexie didn't play any more games. "Take me. Fuck me and mark me. Please."

With a groan, he thrust his swollen cock into her, triggering aftershocks that had her keening mindlessly.

"Now for my turn," he said.

CHAPTER TWENTY-SIX

BURIED to the hilt in her shuddering moistness, Anthony gritted his teeth not to come. Pleasuring her, holding her prisoner and making her beg, all those things combined put him on the edge of his own orgasm. But he well remembered her words. To claim her, and keep her forever, he needed bite her at the moment of orgasm.

With that thought in mind, he moved slowly in her, setting a steady pace. She looked so beautiful and soft beneath him, her cheeks flushed and her lips curved in a sweet smile of pleasure. However, he wanted to see her eyes, read them.

"Look at me," he ordered.

Her green eyes flickered open, her lids heavy with passion, and her gaze aglow with emotion. Staring into her visage, he increased his pace, noting how her breathing hitched and the smell of her arousal clung heavy in the air. He deepened his stroke and her lips parted on a sigh. Her hips gyrated in time with his thrusts, tilting to take him further inside her. He felt his orgasm building, but he strained against it until he felt the walls of her sex begin tightening around him.

"Mine," he growled. He buried his face into her shoulder, licking the skin there, biting only when the tremors of her orgasm rippled along his cock. He sank his teeth into her soft skin and heard her scream his name, her climax suddenly tripling in intensity and launching his own bliss.

The metallic taste of her blood hit his tongue and suddenly a deep hunger invaded him, and he gulped hungrily at her essence. Caught in the throes of a pleasure so intense, he only vaguely noted her cries of pleasure, so intent was he on marking and feeding from her. What seemed like scant seconds later, a growled warning from the newly acquired pet inside his mind made him release her flesh reluctantly. As sanity returned, he suffered a moment's guilt and horror at what he'd just done. *What have I become?* Then he saw the silly smile on her face, and all doubt fled. He'd do and become anything if it meant keeping Lexie.

"I love you." He uttered the words without thinking, and her eyes shot open in shock.

Uncertainty tried to grab him like it had so many times in the past, but he fought it. He loved her, and even if she didn't know it yet or wouldn't admit it, she loved him—and even better, according to the vivid bite-mark on her neck, she belonged to him.

"I—" She never got to finish her sentence, because

the sudden cracking of glass had them both diving off the bed. He stood in front of her protectively, while she went for the jacket on the chair where she pulled out a gun.

"We're under attack."

It was an unnecessary statement on her part because, with his enhanced hearing and senses, Anthony could hear the sounds of battle. He also saw a prime opportunity to try out his new powers.

He ran at the window and dove through the shattered remains.

Lexie's scream of, "No!" followed him as he dropped through the air and hit the ground in a crouch without the slightest jolt or pain. *Cool.*

The wide expanse around him overwhelmed him for a moment with sensory overload. His brain quickly went to work sorting what his five senses noted, and zoomed in on the most important—danger. He sniffed the air, inhaling deep, then turned his head sideways to peer at the darkness. A figure stepped from the shadows and Anthony growled as he recognized the bastard who'd shot Lexie at the conference.

He noticed something else too—the guy had pointed ears.

"What the fuck are you?"

The Spock eared assassin didn't reply, but he raised his gun. In a flash, Anthony reached the attacker and flung his paltry weapon away before grabbing him in a headlock. Then he bit him.

Anthony didn't have time to savor the new unique

flavor of the thug turned victim. Movement from the trees coalesced into more sharp eared freaks.

Anthony thrust the limp body away from him and wiped his mouth before giving them a feral grin. "Who's next?"

Wielding a variety of weapons, and in some cases, just themselves, the invaders rushed him. And then stopped to look for him. With his new found speed, Anthony moved amongst them lightning quick, punching, kicking and tearing at the bastards who'd tried to kill him and almost managed to kill Lexie. His intrigued scientific side noted that while he kept downing them, the bastards kept getting back up.

He also discovered that while newfound strength and powers were great, they didn't prevent injury—even if said wounds healed quickly—and against great numbers, he began to question the wisdom of his decision in facing them alone.

A pointy eared, green skinned creature that made Anthony think of a goblin lunged at him, only to stop with a stunned look before falling face first on the ground. A silver blade stuck out from the back of his head. No sooner did he note this than the crack of a revolver boomed. Anthony looked up to see Lexie had arrived and judging by the glint in her eyes, she was pissed. But not as pissed as he was when he realized how many male eyes had swiveled and regarded her naked form.

And thus did he truly begin to battle in earnest.

CHAPTER TWENTY-SEVEN

LEXIE USED up the ammo in her gun, shooting the attacking Fae in the heads with silver bullets, the only way to bring the sly bastards down and render them out of action for a while. To truly kill one of the immortal ones, she'd require an axe, gas and a lighter. Hopefully, Frederick kept some marshmallows in stock.

Adrenaline pumped through her body, more from the way Anthony dove out of the window than the battle. As she worked her way toward her new mate, she noticed the vamps, including Frederick, had come to join the battle. The Fae risked a lot attacking in such large numbers, not that she could blame them given what she knew of Anthony's success. Unfortunately for them, she was on his side, and as such, they needed to die for trying to harm him.

She got distracted several times by the sight of her geek-turned-alpha fighting. What he lacked in training and finesse, he made up for in raw power. With no prior instruction, he'd managed to bring forth his claws and he used them with devastating effect along with his fangs which she still wasn't sure were vampire or wolf in origin.

She worked her way toward him, taking out the goblins who got in her way—nasty slimy creatures. She hated them as much as mice. When she got within a few feet of Anthony, she yelled. "Don't you ever dare scare me like that again."

Without pausing in his ass kicking of the pair of trolls attacking him, he snarled back. "Get inside, and get some damned clothes on."

She laughed. "Like hell am I leaving you to fight alone."

"How am I supposed to protect you if I'm distracted by your naked body?" he growled as she took aim and fired at one of his assailants between the eyes.

"Get used it to, lover. You're part shifter now. Just wait until I take you to meet my parents. You'll get to see lots of naked people."

He stopped fighting to turn and face her with a pleased look. "You're going to take me to meet them?"

She shot the goblin sneaking up on him before answering. "Well, duh," she said, rolling her eyes. "It's what a girl does when she meets the man of her dreams, falls in love and mates with him."

And that quickly, she found herself swept into his arms. "You love me?"

"Of, course I love you. I wouldn't have let you mark

me if I didn't. Which reminds me, we got interrupted before I returned the favor."

"Well then, shall we adjourn?" He stepped away and crooked his arm at her. Lexie arched a brow and looked around at the dying battlefield.

"Um, don't we need to finish up here?"

Anthony chuckled. "Nah. Let Frederick do the rest. We took care of most of it already. Besides, we've got more important things to do."

They left the scene of chaos, but never made it to bed. Anthony thrust her up against the elevator wall, and as he pounded his dick into her soaking sex, she bit him. She sank her fangs in deep, marking him to show the world that this geek—the most wonderful, sexy and lovable man ever—was all hers.

Forever.

EPILOGUE

THE SWISH OF the apartment door opening had Anthony bounding from bed, stark naked. Lexie didn't immediately follow, opting first to dress herself before going out to rescue Frederick. Anthony held him pinned to the wall by the throat and, while the vampire strived to pry the choking fingers off, he wasn't making any headway.

"Anthony, put him down."

Her lover and mate peered at her over his bare shoulder. "I will, once my former employer and I come to an agreement."

"Former?" Frederick sputtered, his undead face turning red.

"Yes, former. From here on in, we'll be partners."

"Easy for you to say since I'm the one who's expended the funds to set this place up. And if I'm not mistaken, you've taken advantage of the research you were doing for me to enhance yourself."

Anthony dropped Frederick and moved to stand by the large window, unashamed of his body as he stood proudly and stirred her just-sated hunger. "With what I've discovered," her lover said. "You'll make your investment back plus some."

Lexie blanched as his words sank in. "You can't mean to sell the serum. The world couldn't handle that kind of influx of shifters or vamps."

Anthony whirled and shook his head at her with a smile. "Of course not. But what I've discovered will allow us to make money with the big pharmaceuticals healing humans. My nano technology, and what I've learned about the DNA helix, will revolutionize healthcare."

Frederick's eyes brightened and a predatory smile emerged. "We'll make billions. A fantastic plan, but what about my ability to sun walk? I thought you told me that you almost had a solution."

"I do. Lexie, fetch the cage from the solarium."

Lexie, more worried for Frederick's safety than Anthony's at this point, hurried to fetch the cage. She returned with the cage and shook her head as she placed it on the floor in front of the two men. "I think your solution needs more work," she said. "Only one of them survived."

Anthony snorted. "Only one was supposed to. Both were vampire mutated, but only one held the solution to survive direct sunlight."

Frederick's face tightened with such longing Lexie

actually hoped Anthony could help him. After all, the vampire was the reason she'd found her one true love. He deserved some kind of reward for that.

"How soon before you can run some more tests?"

Anthony shrugged. "I can start today. I'll even video-tape the results. When you're satisfied, come to me and I'll administer the serum."

Anthony actually didn't make it to the lab until much later on—first he required breakfast, followed by dessert. Once they did make it down to his lab, Lexie had a smile plastered from ear to ear and a deliciously sore pussy.

TRUE TO HIS WORD, Anthony worked hard the next few days. Becoming an alpha werewolf with some vampire tendencies hadn't diminished his smarts, but rather amplified them.

Frederick took three days before he returned, arriving just before dawn broke. He hesitated before holding out his arm. "How can I be sure, you won't kill me?"

Anthony smirked. "If I wanted to kill you, I'd do it with my bare hands. Lucky for you, I kind of like you. Now stop being a wuss."

"Bossy geek," Frederick muttered as Anthony pricked him, probably harder than necessary, with the needle.

Lexie waited for him to go into convulsions, scream or something, but other than turning more pale than usual, Frederick did nothing untoward.

"Ready to get your first sunburn in a few hundred years?" Anthony asked with a grin.

"I swear, if I melt into a puddle of goo, I'm going to haunt your ass," Frederick grumbled.

"It'll work. Come on."

Lexie held her breath as Anthony opened the door to outside and stepped into the crisp morning air. Dawn was cresting and its soft rays bathed him in a fiery light. She saw Frederick swallow hard, still hidden in the gloom of the hall. With a courage that had to take every ounce of his strength, Frederick straightened his shoulders and took brisk steps to join Anthony, his only hesitation came at the doorway, then he plunged outside.

Lexie followed, a smile breaking free as she saw Frederick, a rapturous expression on his face, twirling in the UV rays that were deadly to every other vampire alive—make that undead.

"It worked. It worked!" Frederick shouted.

"I told you it would," Anthony replied, rolling his eyes. "But, there is one side effect that you should know about."

Frederick stopped his spinning and narrowed his gaze. "What?"

"I couldn't quite cure your vampiric state."

"I should hope not. I like being a vampire. I just didn't want to be stuck in the dark."

"Good. Well, the serum I gave you will not affect your night time vampire abilities, but as for the day..."

Frederick grabbed Anthony and tried to lift him, to no avail. "What did you do to me?" he shouted instead.

"In order to allow you to walk by day, I needed to make you human again." At Frederick's inarticulate cry of rage, Anthony shrugged. "Just when you're in direct sunlight. As soon as you get out of the UV rays you'll go back to your regular vampire self."

As if to test this theory, Frederick ran back into the darkness of the building. Lexie pivoted to watch him and saw his eyes flare red from the shadows.

Anthony laughed. "Hey, it's not that bad. And just think, you'll be able to enjoy regular food again so long as you eat it on a patio."

Frederick stalked back outside and growled. "I liked you better when you were a geek."

Anthony smirked. "You mean when I was a pushover. Tell you what, if you really hate it, then I'll take it away. But take a few days to think about it first. Go, enjoy the sunshine, but try not to get sunburnt."

Frederick leaned his face back and closed his eyes against the rising sun. He sighed. "I still hate you." With those words, he stalked off in the direction of his house, the sunlight making his black hair glint with blue highlights.

Lexie shook her head. "That wasn't nice, lover. You should have warned him about the side effects beforehand."

"Bah," Anthony scoffed. "He would have done it anyway. If you ask me, it's the best of both worlds. Although, I probably should have mentioned the need to start carrying condoms around because another tiny issue is the fact his sperm becomes viable if he makes love by sunlight."

Lexie tried to stifle her laughter, but it bubbled out, and seconds later Anthony joined her. Her cell phone chirped on her hip, and still giggling, Lexie answered it. "Hi, mom. I was going to call you. I'll be coming by this weekend for dinner with my mate."

Her mother's voice squeaked. "What? How?"

"Well, remember that geek job I got injured on? Turns out, a nerdy scientist was just the man I needed to steal my heart." She hung up her phone while her mother was mid squeal and took a step back, preparing to flee, because judging by the look in her mate's eye, she was about to pay for using her nickname for him. *Lucky me.*

THE END

Author's Note: I hope you enjoyed this spicy story. For more awesome stories please visit my website at **EveLanglais.com**

Thank you for reading. ∼ Eve